# First Date

*A novel path to recovery*

**Books by Mark E. Scott**

**A Day in the Life series**
Book 1: Drunk Log
Book 2: First Date


**Coming Soon!**
**A Day in the Life series**
Book 3: Free Will


**For more information**
**visit:** www.SpeakingVolumes.us

# First Date

*A novel path to recovery*

## Mark E. Scott

SPEAKING VOLUMES, LLC
NAPLES, FLORIDA
2023

First Date

ISBN 978-1-64540-840-6

For Nicole

# Acknowledgments

As always, first and foremost I want to thank my agent, Nancy Rosenfeld, for believing in me and never giving up. Her determination is inspiring.

It is impossible to fully express my gratitude to Nicole McCoubrey, my partner and confidante. This book was written during an unbelievably trying time in our lives, and we did not emerge unscathed. But she was always there to listen to my stupid ideas, to read, and to offer an honest point of view. And to wait for me to finish. Thank you, Nicole, for sacrificing so much of our time together and for helping me fulfill a lifelong dream. If I am lucky, I'll have you around for all the books that come after this one.

My thanks also to David Tabatsky, writer, editor, and collaborator. His brain is an idea machine. My undying gratitude to the Central Cincinnati Fiction Writers, for the limitless help and friendship you've all provided. Many, many thanks to Julia Durso, who leant me her nursing expertise in ways great and small and helped make Jack and Aria's time in the hospital a believable experience. My heartfelt thanks to my friend Paul Gaitan, who made his basement available to me and my dog whenever I needed a place to write this book. I'm unbelievably lucky to have the support of my family, and always have been. Iris, Tim, Rick, Missy, Hannah, Jake, and Lydia. Thank you all for putting up with this. Thank you to Officer Bill Springer (Retired) for making sure I followed procedure. A HUGE thanks to Elizabeth Mariner, my second editor. You've made this book better and never lost my voice. Your commitment was astounding. Finally, I want to thank Kurt and Erica Mueller at Speaking Volumes, from whom I keep learning and whose support made this possible.

# Chapter One

## Out of the Frying Pan

Jack was supposed to be dead by now. The jump off the bridge was *supposed* to kill him. But it didn't. In fact, the jump off the bridge didn't kill either of them.

But there was Aria, pulling on his hand, trying to drag him up and out of the water. It was freezing cold and snowing and she figured the ground was slippery, but was surprised when it was even softer than she expected and her foot sank in the frigid muck of the riverbank. Now stuck in place, she willed herself not to move until she believed Jack was secure, felt him move toward her. Standing in the shallow water, he seemed dazed, and she wasn't sure if her efforts to pull him away from the edge of the river were really having an effect.

When Jack did start moving, so did Aria. Or at least she tried to. Her right foot, the one she was using as an anchor, was stuck, and as soon as she moved her left foot, she began to slip in the mud. So she stopped. Looking down, she could see her foot and part of her calf buried under eight inches of river detritus, dirt, and mystery muck. Though the Ohio River was cleaner than it had been in years, swimming in it was generally not recommended. Certainly not in the dead of winter, though health concerns were not a priority for Jack when he decided on his jumping-off point.

Jack and Aria were banged up, but the snow-filtered glow from the exterior lights of the nearby Cincinnati Bengals football stadium was not quite enough for them to see the blood from their wounds, or even if there was any blood. Neither had said a word since they'd slammed into the anchored coal barge—a painful event, but a fortunate one if living was the objective. The parked barge arrested their momentum in the powerful current and saved them from being pulled further downstream.

Aria was the first to break through the shock-induced silence.

"Jack, I need your help. My foot is buried."

Aria continued to grasp his hand, fearing the river might take him if she let go, fearing he might *want* to let go.

"I'm afraid if I pull too hard, I'll lose my shoe. Help me."

Aria's words slurred, teeth chattering from the cold invading her skin through soaked clothes. She wondered which was having more effect on her ability to speak clearly, the cold or all the alcohol she'd consumed before falling off the bridge.

Jack hadn't said a word since colliding with the barge, and wasn't sure what words would come out of his mouth, or even if he was able to open it. His brain was still processing the last ten minutes, piecing together the moments leading to him jumping off the bridge after Aria slipped over the rail, but comprehended enough of what Aria said to get down on his knees to help release her foot and shoe from the icy crud. But, since one of his hands was still holding one of hers, he had limited ability to dig into the freezing muck.

*Don't let go. No matter what, do not let go.*

Jack was determined to keep his grip intact as he attempted to free her shoe with one hand. He was shaken and confused about why she was there in the river with him, an outcome he'd never considered. His intent had been to kill himself, but now his only thought was to cling to Aria for dear life.

"Jack . . . my foot."

Aria's voice penetrated his muddled mind and he allowed his gaze to float up to her face. He tried to speak, but still no words would come. The plunge into the icy river had a sobering effect, but it was fleeting, and he remembered the copious amount of alcohol he'd consumed in the hours prior to the jump. He wanted to ask Aria if she was okay, if she was hurt, but his voice abandoned him. Even his own pain didn't quite register. Instead, he nodded at his captive hand and, reluctantly, they both let go.

Jack, now with both hands free, plunged them directly into the hole Aria's foot had created and worked them down her leg until he could feel her hiking boot. As he came out of his daze, he felt suddenly thrilled to be this close to her, so intimately, even under these circumstances.

*We haven't been this close since we kissed earlier this year.*

Both of them were aware of this, but in passing, as the elements began to take their toll. The night their lips met they were separated by a bar, the copper-covered wood keeping them a couple feet apart, too far for anything but a kiss. Now, she was letting him touch her, even if it was only to assist in releasing her foot from nature's icy grip. But in that moment Jack did not feel the extreme cold on his hands and arms, despite the chilled mud being jammed into his coat sleeves. Moments later her boot released from the wet soil with a resounding 'THWUCK,' leaving Jack feeling triumphant.

"Ow!"

Jack flinched, afraid he'd hurt her.

"It's okay. I'm alright. Thank you, Jack."

He stood, successful in his labors, and was so close to her she could have, should have, put her arms around him, but she didn't. It was a confusing moment, another in a succession of confusing moments that preceded Aria discovering Jack on the bridge. Neither of them could rewind those moments now, not yet at least, as they had a more pressing issue to deal with—survival.

Aria took a few backward steps, slipped on some ice, steadied herself and reached out her hand again, inviting Jack to take it.

"We should get away from this mud."

Jack took the offering, transferring some of the mud from his hand to hers, and allowed her to lead him the few steps to stiffer ground. He marveled at her ability to form words, even as her teeth continued to chatter.

*I've got words. Why can't I get them out of my mouth?*

Aria stopped moving, but didn't release Jack's hand from hers or his eyes from her gaze.

She shivered. "Warm. We should try to get warm."

Jack nodded and forced a word from his mouth. "Yes."

*Dumbass. You know how to talk.*

The words *were* starting to come, deep from within, but not easily.

Aria continued to direct. "Let's huddle up for a little bit and see if we can get warm."

As the words left her lips, she was overcome by a violent coughing fit as her body worked to expel river water from her lungs. The fit was sufficiently ferocious to force her to her knees, and Jack found himself patting her back in a weak, useless attempt to provide assistance.

As the coughing subsided, it occurred to Jack that he wanted nothing more than to 'huddle up' with Aria, but felt they should move further from the river. It also occurred to him that sitting in the freezing cold may be counterproductive to the goal of increasing body temperatures, but he said nothing, and not just because he still lacked the power of speech. There was no reason to believe any ideas of his would work out better than hers, and he'd already tried to kill her once, albeit accidentally. Plus, they were soaked through and at the moment Aria was in no condition to scrabble around a dark, slippery riverbank.

*How much worse could it be to sit in some snow?*

Aria sat first, pulling Jack gently down with her to a seated position, crisscross applesauce, facing each other. Had either been a tad more sober they might have looked for something, natural or manmade, to shelter them from the wind. But the alcohol had begun to reassert itself, slowing their thoughts.

Jack heard Aria grunt in pain as she lowered herself to a seated position. He took inventory of his own bangs and bruises and, miraculously, didn't think he was badly hurt, or at least nothing felt broken, despite his plan to be dead by now. Aria also seemed to be in one piece, though he took a mental note to ask as soon as he was able. Seated across from her, however, she appeared to be in no worse shape.

Now tantalizingly close, Jack made a clumsy attempt to get even closer, to embrace. To his delight, Aria responded in kind, but their somewhat awkward attempts to envelop one another, combined with the fact they had yet to release the hand of the other, only increased the awkwardness.

"Hold on, Jack, let me try something."

She was taking control.

Aria let go of Jack's hand and slid closer, covering the remaining inches between them and wrapping her legs around Jack's waist. They were now as close as they could be, closer than they had ever been. He took a breath to capture the moment, to enjoy the feel of this closeness, before unbuttoning his coat and wrapping it around her, covering as much of her torso as possible. Pulling hard on the fabric, he managed to get it stretched over her arms and about a third of her back and within moments they could feel the heat building between them.

Underneath his coat, Jack felt Aria's arms enclose him.

He was more alert than he had in a long time. Not exactly sober, but he felt his body recovering from the shock of what he'd just been through and, in fact, something much deeper was coming alive, though he wasn't ready to give it a name.

Aria released Jack just long enough to unbutton her own, soaked, jacket.

*It's actually Tracy's coat,* she reminded herself. *At least it was until about an hour ago. Doubt she'll want it back now.*

Aria told herself that opening her coat would increase the efficiency of their shared body heat. Silly, she thought. Under the circumstances, removing layers of clothing to get closer to Jack didn't need to be rationalized, or justified, or explained to anyone.

They sat together in the stillness of the snowfall, trying hard not to disturb this moment they'd accidentally created. Seconds passed into minutes, and before long Aria's teeth stopped chattering and she rested her head on Jack's shoulder. They were getting warmer with each passing minute and neither could find a reason to move, no reason to break the spell.

"You know, Jack. If you wanted to go on a date, all you had to do was ask." Her voice was a whisper in Jack's ear. "I promise I would have said yes."

Aria's words were lighthearted, but her admission pulled him back to the sequence of events that ended with her slipping on an icy section of bridge walkway, falling over the rail, and him jumping in behind her.

The potential consequences of their actions were beginning to trickle into their brains. In spite of that duress, or perhaps because of it, neither let go of the other. Even as their minds began to race, flip-flopping from one image to another, Jack and Aria found their close physical proximity nothing short of marvelous, but Aria had a question.

"Jack, what the hell just happened?"

The question was apropos, but Jack did not attempt a response. He wasn't sure he had the right answer and, besides, speaking still posed a problem. Though he could piece together the sequence of events that concluded with him and Aria in the river, at that moment he couldn't fully grasp what *happened.*

"We could have died, you know?" Her head was still on his shoulder.

*Well . . . that was the plan. I mean . . . for me anyway. You kind of fucked it up. But I'm glad you did. I think . . .*

Jack kept his mouth shut, deciding not to speak until his brain was able to process something coherent, something that would make sense to both of them. He managed, however, to vocalize the following:

"Hmmm."

*One minute I'm on my way to kill myself, and the next I'm clinging to the woman of my . . . what? My dreams? My hopes? So weird . . .*

The throaty sound Jack managed to emit was enough to satisfy Aria, at least for the moment. She didn't want to think too much. She was still comfortable in the heat they were sharing, her head still on his shoulder. Plus, she figured the noise indicated he was thinking about her question, and that was all she needed to know for now. She also figured Jack had every right to ask the same question of her, that she was complicit in what she would soon begin referring to as "the incident," and that it would make sense for her to go ahead and begin trying to piece things together on her own, instead of just waiting for

Jack to answer the question for her. The bonus was that, for her brain to work on the problem, she didn't have to move.

But a thought jerked her head upright.

"Jack, your phone."

He shook his head.

"You don't have it?"

He shook his head again. Aria laid her head back on his shoulder, recalling the multiple voicemails she'd left him earlier in the evening. But Jack had purposely left his phone on the kitchen island before leaving his apartment, not wanting any of its distractions as he drank and wrote himself toward a suicide which, given his failure to actually complete the act, he now reclassified as an *attempt*.

While each silently worked through the events of the evening, and especially the last half-hour, something started creeping into their moment of intimacy, something unexpected and earthy. It was the smell. Now that things had calmed, now that they were both safely out of the river and keeping each other warm, the sensory world began to intrude, and there was definitely a smell. An unpleasant smell. On the positive side, the stench activated Jack's speech center.

"Wow, I think my coat picked up something smelly. Shit."

"Shit? You think it's shit?" Aria lifted her head and smiled. "Actual shit?"

Jack almost laughed. "From the river, I mean. I think I got a good scraping while we were in the water."

Jack was amazed so many words were coming out of his mouth all at once, and that they sounded somewhat normal. It seemed all that was necessary to reconnect with his speech center was to stop thinking. But his brain kept working in the background, and was busy performing an independent autopsy of the *attempt*. Jack's noodle was figuring out where he went wrong, figuring out what he'd have to correct to make the *attempt* successful. When he became aware of what his mind was up to, he told it not to obsess on his failure. That could come later.

*Be in the moment.*

Aria looked directly at Jack. "I don't think I smell any better."

Jack smiled, quietly agreeing. "Are you ok?"

Now prompted, it was Aria's turn to perform a comprehensive once-over, letting her mind feel around her body to determine if anything hurt or felt out of sorts. She concluded there was plenty of pain but, like Jack, believed nothing was broken. Even the butterfly stitches on her forehead, the ones she'd earned earlier that evening after falling off the curb, survived the swim.

"Yeah, actually. I think I'm okay, Jack, but it's too dark to see anything. How about you?"

"I think I'm scraped up, for sure, but I can't see anything either."

Jack continued to hold his reeking pea coat around Aria and her legs remained wrapped around him. They were warm, the cold having yet to penetrate their makeshift protective cloak. What *was* managing to creep in, other than the stench, was that something big had happened, or *not* happened.

Jack vocalized his disappointment. "Well, at least now I know that the endgame to my plan was flawed."

The statement startled Aria but she hid her reaction. "What do you mean?"

"I mean, jeez, my whole deal was that I was going to end it all tonight by throwing myself off that bridge."

"Because of Troy?" Aria softened her voice at the mention of Jack's nephew.

"Exactly. It's been a year since the accident. I had a plan. Just not a good one, I guess."

Jack's voice was matter-of-fact, a tone that neither frightened nor angered Aria. In fact, she suppressed a laugh, believing it inappropriate, considering they actually could have both died. But, she told herself, she wasn't laughing at the tragedy of Troy's death, or Jack's level of responsibility for it. She was laughing at the ridiculousness of his level-headed disappointment in himself.

"Well, Jack, just where do you think you screwed up?"

Before Jack had a chance to register Aria's sarcasm, his engineer brain kicked in to answer the question.

"Well, for starters I'd say the bridge wasn't high enough off the water. It's only about 70 or 80 feet above the surface of the water and, really, you need at least 150 feet to be sure of the outcome. I guess I thought I'd get lucky." Jack paused while he pondered the miscalculation. "I mean, look, we're both still alive, which, you know, I'm super-glad we survived and all. I think my point is that, since we did both survive, that I actually failed."

Aria laughed again, the moment so absurd the only reason she was able to take it seriously was that, years before, her sister Steffi actually succeeded where Jack had failed.

"Listen, Jack, I'm *super*-glad we survived, too. And, right now, even sitting with you in the cold, well, being alive doesn't feel so bad. Better than the alternative." She tried to move closer, but kept her nose as far from his coat as possible.

Jack nodded. "Mmm."

Jack thought, of course she was right. This was better, this moment of sitting on the cold ground, soaking wet, wrapped up with each other. It was far better than the alternative. Mostly.

Aria's voice floated up from beneath his chin. "I was afraid I wouldn't find you in time."

Jack let the idea of Aria spending her evening searching for him sink in. He could make out Aria's face in the gloom and despite her sodden appearance, she looked beautiful and peaceful, snowflakes melting silently on her red cheeks. It felt good to have her in his arms.

Aria continued. "Remember what I told you on the bridge? About how I got a look in your notebook and got worried about you? The part I read didn't say anything about killing yourself but I was still afraid you were going to do something stupid, you know, something like jumping off a bridge. I wanted to stop you."

It was Jack's turn to laugh, but not at Aria. He laughed at how absurd their current predicament appeared, at how laughable it was that they would end up where they were, together. All because of a stupid wire bound notebook.

He smiled at her. "How'd that work out for you?"

Aria put her warm hands on Jack's cold cheeks and he winced. "Ooh. Sorry. I didn't see the bruise."

"Well, could be worse."

Aria removed her hands from Jack's face and hid them back under his coat before the wind had a chance to suck all the heat from them.

Jack had not thought about the notebook, the Drunk Log, since right before jumping into the river after Aria. It contained his thoughts and memories of his nephew, Troy, and other things he thought worthy of comment. It was supposed to have been safely crammed between two blocks of the bridge's north tower *before* he went into the water. Now, he had to think. Did he manage to get it into a chink in the tower's mortar before Aria fell? Was it in his hand when he jumped? His coat?

Then he remembered: He'd slid the notebook into his back pocket when Aria found him on the bridge, right before she slipped and careened over the handrail. Right before he jumped in after her. If he had the notebook, it would be in his back pocket.

Jack now felt anxious about where it may have disappeared and, in a worse-case scenario, how far it may have traveled in the river.

"Sorry, Aria. I need my hand for a sec. I need to check if the log is in my pocket."

"You need it now? Do I have to move? I think I found the perfect position."

"Um, maybe a little. I need to know if I've still got it. I just need to check my back pocket."

Aria sensed Jack's urgency. "No, it's ok. I'll check for you. Don't move. You're keeping me warm."

Aria slid her hands down Jack's back. He said nothing, allowing them to work their way down to where the notebook should be. Despite the numbness having spread through his posterior, there was no mistaking the placement of Aria's hands, the warmth they generated, or the fact that she was quite thorough in her search.

"I'm sorry, Jack. The notebook isn't in your pocket."

The log was gone.

"Are you sure?"

"It isn't there."

Jack's anxiety was in danger of becoming a full-fledged panic. The log had become important to him, vital, in fact, but this had developed stealthily, without Jack recognizing the grip it had on him. He'd spent a year with the guilt of Troy's death and whatever had poured out of him onto the pages of the college-ruled notebook had taken on an unexpected significance. He'd not meant the log to be for him, had not meant to write something for himself. It was supposed to be read by someone else, later. It was meant to be found *after*. It was meant for his family, his parents, his sister and brother-in-law. He meant it as an explanation, an apology to anyone who claimed to love him, even if they may not have been too broken up had Jack's plan succeeded. At least that's the idea Jack lived with for a year. And he managed to pour it all into the notebook.

Aria watched those thoughts traverse Jack's face, without knowing exactly what they were. She nodded in a quiet effort to be reassuring about things she didn't yet understand.

Jack wondered if the notebook was close to them, on the riverbank but closer to the water.

It was certainly possible. The current had carried them to the rear end of a barge, into an eddy and, in the process, nearly spit them out of the river. It could easily have done the same to the notebook. He was just about to ask Aria if she would help him look for it, but while Jack had been sounding his internal alarm over the loss of the log, Aria had been considering what might happen next and what kind of trouble they might be in. She was thinking about how to get them safely home, about keeping secrets.

"Jack, I'm sorry about the log, but we've got something else to think about." Aria paused to organize her thoughts. "I'm thinking we're going to have to get home, as best we can, and not tell anyone about what we just did, or anything about what we've been doing all night."

Jack nodded his understanding while Aria continued.

"If we do then you'll probably end up in the looney bin."

Until that moment, Jack had not put any thought into the aftermath of his actions. After all, he hadn't planned to be around for the aftermath, but she made sense.

"You're right. What's our next move?"

"Okay, let's start simple. Let's stand up."

But standing was not as simple as she'd hoped. Sitting motionless, their muscles and joints had nearly frozen in place. Aria untangled herself from Jack and, with some effort, managed to stand. Now overconfident, she grabbed Jack's hand and took a step toward the stadium, only to fall back on Jack.

"Maybe just standing for a minute?" he said.

Aria nodded, frustrated, but also glad to be stuck alone with Jack a little longer. "Good idea."

The red and blue flashing lights, however, caught their attention.

# Chapter Two

## Ghosts and Gators

Sergeant Timothy Thompson, a twenty-year veteran of the Hamilton County Sheriff's Department, was unusually excited to get the call from dispatch. A 911 operator was contacted by a man driving through an empty surface lot behind the Bengals stadium and claimed to have seen something crawl out of the water, and that the thing, or things, *appeared* to be human.

However, Sergeant Thompson was also told that the caller wasn't actually 100 percent sure about the purported humanity of the creatures he'd spotted crawling out of the river and, upon further evaluation, speculated that whatever was taking a break from river life was quite possibly not human at all and was, in all likelihood, an alligator, or maybe even a lungfish. The caller declined to say what he was doing in an empty, snowy parking lot at midnight, leaving Thompson and the dispatcher to hypothesize. He also declined to wait for the authorities, mumbling something about the snow before hanging up.

The deputy shared a good laugh with the dispatcher over the ridiculousness of the excitable caller, even as he calculated his odds of finding an alligator on the shores of a midwestern river in winter.

*But what, exactly, is a lungfish?*

Sergeant Thompson recalled something from a National Geographic special he'd watched with his wife, but didn't remember if lungfish were dangerous or even how big they could get. He reflexively fingered his sidearm, just in case.

Thompson was excited to be excited. Thus far the night had been rather monotonous. The snow had seen to that. Most of the calls he'd received that evening pertained to automobiles bouncing off other automobiles, as well as telephone poles, street signs, and mailboxes— a rather boring bit of policing for a practiced professional such as himself.

Arriving near the scene of the speculative alligator sighting, Sergeant Thompson parked and left the flashers on. It occurred to him that finding a lungfish would actually be more interesting than finding an alligator, but wasn't sure a lungfish's chances of survival in the cold river were any better than an alligator's.

*Aren't those things from Africa or somewhere?*

Certainly, if it did exist, the lungfish would be less dangerous than an alligator, or so he assumed. In any case, he didn't want either one of them near his house, which was less than two miles away.

"Do you see the lights?"

"I do."

There was a tone to Aria's voice. It was panic. He remembered the sound of it from some of the rescue workers the day of the accident with Troy.

"Do you think we can make a run for it?" Her voice was a little shaky, and not because of the cold.

Though Aria had been working on formulating their escape plan, their ability to actually run was still very much in doubt. When the sheriff's car appeared they were still just standing, waiting for the blood flow to return to their legs. Her hope was that, despite the darkness and a slight deficit of geographical knowledge, they could work their way out of this predicament on their own. She believed, or at least hoped, they could pick their way off the riverbank and get home despite the cold seeping into their clothes and their lack of motorized transport. She tried to convince herself they really weren't that far from where they lived and, under normal circumstances, the walk would have taken no more than 45 minutes.

Now, Aria's plan was being foiled by the arrival of the authorities, and for her the cops posed a bigger problem than just getting arrested for jumping off a bridge. She knew any encounter would lead to questions and feared her name would come up in their system. There would be an official report. Background checks were in the offing.

*We should want to be rescued, right?*

But she did not want to be rescued, or to have anything to do with the cops at all.

Other than his current lack of mobility, Jack, for his part, could find no reason to object to Aria's desire to make a run for it. But the few practice steps he attempted ended with him back on his hands and knees.

"Well, damn, my legs aren't cooperating." Jack didn't mention the sharp pain, the lightning bolt in his hip, the constant reminder of his sin.

Aria plopped down close to Jack; she patted her thighs in an attempt to increase blood flow.

"Yeah, wow. Oh, jeez, mine are numb. But we've really got to move. I can't have anything to do with the cops."

The cruiser's torch searched the darkness.

Thompson turned on the hood-mounted searchlight and, despite the bad angle caused by his elevation relative to the river, tried to give the shoreline a good once-over to see if anything interesting stood out. Nothing did. The things he could identify in the light were not strange or foreign to him. He saw a coal barge lashed to some cleats mounted

17

on cement pilings, the water lapping against the floating container. He saw the snow gathering on its uncovered load. He saw trees and bushes poking out below the snow-covered grass off the edge of the parking lot. He could see Kentucky across the river.

He touched his sidearm again.

It was easy for him to identify the things he was used to seeing near the river, even things onto which one couldn't necessarily pin a label, but looked normal just the same. Things like humps of rock and dirt, or of driftwood and vegetation, or all of the above. Tonight, all the humps were covered in snow, and what Thompson *didn't* see were humps that looked like alligators.

The lights had interrupted their attempt to reanimate, to move. and Jack understood that he and Aria couldn't just huddle in the cold all night, no matter how much they were lost in each other. He also understood that she was more anxious than he to avoid contact with whoever was in charge of the searchlight.

*Eventually we will freeze to death, or at least catch a really bad cold. Or maybe Ohio River cholera. Is that a thing?*

Jack looked around for a shelter, someplace to hide from the wind as well as the cops. There were ample hiding opportunities close by, so he chose one that might protect them from the light as well as the wind, but they both needed to move.

"Aria, let's see if we can get behind that pile of rocks. The cop won't be able to see us over there."

"Ok."

Jack reached across to Aria and was able to get his arms under her shoulders, helping to lift her from a seated position, and they rose from the ground together.

Thompson didn't immediately recognize the two human beings sitting near the edge of the river. They, like the humps, sported a layer of snow, helping them to blend in with their surroundings. Even while employing his searchlight he found nothing he could immediately identify as something that didn't belong. At least not right away.

Staring into the distance, sweeping the torch this way and that, it took Thompson's eyes a moment to detect the movement. One of the humps was levitating off the ground, floating skyward. Startled, his hand jerked a hair, just enough to move the spotlight off the suddenly-animated mound of God-knows-what. Methodically, he inched the torch back to the kinetic mass he'd initially believed to be a heap of driftwood and vegetation, left behind by a spring flood, now choked with dead weeds and fallen leaves. Or was it an alligator?

*Not an alligator. People.*

There was disappointment in the revelation. Certainly, had the 911 caller not suggested the possibility of discovering an ancient, apex predator within his call area, the sergeant's expectations would have been more in line with the reality unfolding in the blinding glare of his searchlight.

*Two drunks on a Friday night.*

Allowing himself just a moment of disenchantment, the experienced peace officer grabbed his megaphone and aimed it at the two human beings, who were now, as far as he could determine, just standing there staring at him.

"Excuse me."

The Sergeant's voice blared from the loudspeaker, but received no reaction. He checked the volume, and was assured the volume was sufficiently high before he again targeted the drunks with his amplified voice.

Jack and Aria heard the voice, knew from where it was coming and knew they'd been identified.

"Jeez."

Aria rolled her eyes. Jack could see her expression in the blazing torchlight. They were standing, frozen in place, rendered immobile by the light and the *voice*, a pair of frightened rabbits in front of an oncoming car. Jack moved first.

"Pssst! C'mon over here."

"Excuse me. People on the riverbank. Can you hear me?"

This time, the wraiths reacted to the voice booming from the edge of the parking lot above. Initially they stopped moving, and appeared to turn toward him, toward the sound of his voice and the brutal light. Then, inexplicably, they ducked behind an *actual* hump of snow-covered flotsam, as if he wouldn't notice. Thompson had seen this behavior before, mostly in the intoxicated, and was more aggrieved than surprised.

"Jack? Don't you think he saw us squat down back here?"

Thompson's voice boomed again. "People hiding behind the clump, please join me up here in the parking lot."

Jack nodded.

"Yup. I definitely think he saw us."

Aria was still willing to try and make a getaway, even though she and Jack were clearly impaired. And she wasn't yet ready to explain to Jack why she was desperate to avoid the cops. It was a story of which she wasn't proud and the longer she could put it off the better. But Jack was thinking rationally.

20

"I hate saying this, Aria, but I guess we go up there. I mean, we didn't do anything wrong, right?"

Aria thought for a moment. "Agreed. At least I don't think we did."

"Exactly. Besides, who's to say what's right and wrong?" Jack tried to lighten the mood.

Aria played along, suddenly feeling blithe. "Yeah. I mean, he's a cop, probably? Not a philosopher."

Jack looked up the hill. "And he doesn't look like a priest, at least not from here."

"Or a lawyer."

"Definitely not a lawyer."

"What's the worst thing that can happen?" Aria took a moment to consider all of the potentially terrible outcomes, dismissed them all, and convinced herself things would turn out in their favor. "Okay, maybe you're right. We're freezing anyway."

She was right about the freezing. From the moment they emerged from their coat cocoon, the wind lashed them and their wet clothes with cold, snowy gusts. Even if the cops hadn't arrived on the scene, they were unsure how long they could last.

Hand in hand, they started to climb up the embankment, around trees and bushes and over rocks to the patiently waiting sergeant and his car. It was difficult and dangerous for the couple, shaken and drunk, the searchlight casting confusing shadows. Finally, Jack and Aria were close enough to the deputy that he no longer needed to amplify his voice.

"You two need a rope?"

Without waiting for an answer, Thompson went to the trunk of his cruiser, pulled out a rope, and fastened it to the push bar on the front of the squad car. He tossed the loose end down to Jack and Aria.

Thompson's aim was true, and a few moments later Jack and Aria were able to scrabble their way up the embankment using the rope in combination with bushes, branches and marginal assistance from the deputy. They stood before Thompson, warmer from the effort but still wet through.

"Well, I'll be honest with you two. I was hoping for alligators. Or lungfish."

Jack and Aria looked at each other, not sure whether to laugh or make a run for it. Sergeant Thompson leaned in to get a better look at them and immediately stepped back.

"Wow, you two reek."

# Chapter Three

## Love and Lies

Sergeant Thompson waited patiently, watching the human clumps crawl up the hill to his perch in the parking lot. Jack and Aria were standing in front of him when Deputy Tommie Lane pulled his cruiser in behind the sergeant's. Immediately after, an ambulance carrying three EMTs pulled in as well. The ambulance had been dispatched shortly after Thompson, with the anticipation that whoever was in the river probably required medical assistance.

Aria and Jack found themselves in the parking lot, out of breath and outnumbered more than two-to-one by emergency personnel. Hands clasped, they'd come to a halt in front of the sergeant's cruiser and handed him their end of the rope, which the deputy took and tossed onto the hood of the car. They were shivering, sore and clueless as to what would happen next. If the fall and the cold and the snow and mud hadn't sobered them, the struggle to climb the embankment certainly had, at least temporarily.

They nodded to express their thanks to Thompson and received a nod and a shrug in return, as if saving people from the river were an everyday occurrence. The three were standing still, but were surrounded by the newcomers pacing around them, unsure how to jump into whatever was happening between Sergeant Thompson and the civilians.

Thompson, having already weighed in on the status of their hygiene, stayed focused on the young couple. "Well, now. What have you two got to say for yourselves?"

Aria and Jack looked at each other, unsure how to respond. To Jack, the tone of the deputy's voice reminded him of an adult scolding a child, and he thought the deputy might have meant it as a joke. He was, however, close to formulating an answer when Deputy Lane intervened.

"What have we got here, Tim?"

Thompson found his co-worker's intrusion something of a nuisance. He was never in a mood to be questioned by an underling, but he hid his annoyance, at least for the moment.

"Well, from what I was told by dispatch, what we've got is a couple of alligators."

Lane had heard the same report from the dispatcher, and, like Thompson, responded to the call on the off chance there might really be alligators crawling out of the Ohio River. Also like Thompson, he was disappointed to find two normal-looking humans, but thought it unprofessional to let them know that; Aria and Jack quietly assumed they were the alligators in question.

"Can I have a word, Tim?"

The two Sheriffs moved a few steps away, toward the ambulance. As far as Aria and Jack could tell, they were in a confab with two of the paramedics—Connor and Samantha, according to their stitched name tags—who had descended from the rear of the ambulance.

Aria and Jack, now abandoned by their new friend, took the opportunity to move closer to one another, irrationally believing the other might disappear the moment they let go. They didn't speak to each other or the cops. They couldn't. The situation was too disconcerting, at least at the moment. If they had any expectations about how their dealings with the cops would unfold, those expectations had been thoroughly flushed during the chilly, slippery hike up the hillside.

Standing next to each other in the cold and snow, they waited for their brains to catch up, to start providing them with useful instructions, or at least the ability to converse coherently. The strain of crawling up the hill, clinging to the rope and each other, had exhausted them.

One thing *was* working, however: their ability to shiver. Standing by the police car, freezing wind whipping wet clothes, no longer sharing each other's heat, their bodies attempted to warm themselves by shaking violently.

The paramedic, Samantha, or Sam, as she preferred, was the first to notice their discomfort. She broke away from the colloquy with the officers and her partner to retrieve some blankets from the back of the ambulance.

"Here you go, you two. These should help. Let's see if we can't get you into one of these cars and get you warmed up before we check you for injuries. You look pretty banged up."

Aria and Jack nodded in thanks, donning the thick, gray blankets while Sam turned her attention back to Sergeant Thompson.

"Tim, can these two sit in your back seat to get warm?"

Sergeant Thompson was conflicted. He preferred not to have the stinky couple in his cruiser, but simultaneously did not want them to die of exposure.

"Sure, Sam, if they don't bleed all over it. I just had it cleaned."

The attempt at humor fell flat and Sergeant Thompson walked Jack and Aria back to his vehicle, engine still running, and opened the back door.

"By the way, what do I call you two?"

Aria found her voice first.

"Aria. And this is Jack."

Jack nodded in agreement.

*Jack is my name, for sure.*

"Yes, Jack. Jack is my name."

Sergeant Thompson stared at Jack in polite silence until he was sure he was finished nodding and saying his name.

"Well, Aria and Jack, I mean no harm, as we presume you are innocent until proven guilty, but for obvious reasons I have to pat you down before I let you into my car. Ladies first, please."

Their brains still frozen, the need for a pat down was not immediately obvious to Jack and Aria, but they complied regardless. They really had no choice. If they wanted to get warm, which they desperately did, they would have to put up with the protocol. The pat-down was a first for Jack, and he felt a tinge of embarrassment as Sheriff Thompson went about his business. Aria felt the same tinge. It was her second pat-down, but she was not inclined to point this out. For both of them, however, the promise of basking in a warm car was enough to overcome their discomfort. Jack and Aria tried not to react when the officer ran his hands over a bad bruise or apparent cut and, for his part, Sergeant Thompson was hesitant to expose himself to the smell or to get his hands covered in mud, so the inspection was as cursory as possible.

Her search completed, Aria waited, silently willing the Sheriff to finish quickly with Jack so they could climb into the cruiser, her patience by the rush of warm air escaping from the open passenger door.

The whole pat down took less than a minute and, once again covered in blankets, they were soon basking in the blasting heat. They were soaked through, but the heat penetrated their clothes, drying them little by little. The moisture, once released from their garments, rose to fog the windows and they began to thaw and relax. Within minutes they began to nod off as the adrenaline from the initial encounter with the police began to wane, allowing the leftover alcohol in their systems to reassert itself.

A sharp sound on the window startled them back to relative alertness. Officer Lane was rapping on the glass with his flashlight.

"Hey, you two. Don't get too comfortable in there. We have questions and the EMTs need to check you out."

"Jack, what are we going to tell them?"

He knew what she was asking. After all, their little tour of the river and its environs was definitely something the police would be interested in hearing about and, given their current circumstances, Jack had decided the best alternative was to lie their asses off.

But, first they needed to coordinate the lie. Should they be interviewed separately, it was vital they be on the same page, that their individual recitations of what happened on the bridge and in the river sound remarkably similar.

And they *were* going to get asked. There was no doubt of that. There was no way the cops were going to just give them a ride home, as they would a couple of lost children, without finding out why they were on the riverbank in the first place.

*We're stuck in shit here. Again.*

The deputies were going to get to the bottom of things, or at least try to get to the bottom of things. It was their job, after all.

For his part, Jack had all kinds of great ideas floating around in his head about what they could say with regard to the whole falling-off-the-bridge scenario, but he was more interested in what Aria might have to say on the topic. Thus far, he had not known her to be at a loss for words or ideas, so while they were alone he took the opportunity to pick her brain.

"Listen, my idea on the whole thing is pretty straightforward, but I want to know what are you thinking?"

"You mean about what we should tell them about the bridge?"

Aria's grogginess was wearing off and she wanted to make sure they were talking about the same thing. And the *other* topic was still waiting in the wings, the one she had avoided thus far. She rubbed her throbbing temples.

Jack smiled. "Yes, exactly."

Aria looked over at Jack. "Okay, well, I'm thinking we should just lie about it."

Officer Lane hit the window with his flashlight again.

"One second!" Jack elevated his voice to be heard through the glass and turned back to Aria. "I couldn't agree more. But we need to decide what our lie will be. We need to tell the same lie."

Aria dove in, excited to trade ideas. "Okay, okay. Of course. Something simple, I think. Something easy to remember, like, what if we tell them we were on a date, you know, and we were walking across the bridge to go to a bar in Kentucky? That's what people in Cincinnati do on a first date. They go to Kentucky, right? So exotic. What do you think?"

"Yes. Okay, good. I'm not sure how exotic Kentucky is, but I like it. Plus, I like the idea of us being on a date."

Jack paused, waiting for Aria's reaction.

"I like that too, Jack. Our first date."

She smiled at him through the flashes of light emitted by the near-by emergency vehicles.

Officer Lane leaned in toward the foggy window, trying to spy Jack and Aria as he tapped his wristwatch.

Jack smiled again. Notwithstanding his current circumstance—sitting in the back of a police car on a freezing cold night after jumping off a bridge to facilitate his own suicide—he was the happiest he'd been in a year.

"And I assume we're avoiding the 'suicide' topic altogether, correct?"

"Absolutely. Telling them about that would be the worst idea we've had all night. And, let's be honest, Jack, we've set a pretty low bar for bad ideas." Aria lowered her voice, as if one of the cops was sitting in the car with them, and laughed at herself, silently recounting the myriad bad ideas that had carried them to that moment. "But, Jack, we will have to talk about it, you know . . . eventually. Sometime after we get through all this."

*And we've got something else to talk about, too.*

Jack felt his face flush with the idea it might be necessary to talk to someone, especially Aria, about what had, only hours before, been his singular goal.

"Uh, yeah, I know, Aria. And I will, or we will . . . eventually. I just don't want to bring it up with these guys. It'll become a whole big thing. It'll become something we can't control, and I don't know what happens, you know, if that happens."

Aria turned toward Jack, hugged him, and kissed him on the cheek.

"You're safe with me, Jack."

"I know." He held the hug for a moment but had something more on his mind. "What about the drinking?"

"What do you mean? Do you think they'll test us?"

"Not sure. We weren't driving, Aria. It's not illegal to drink and walk onto a bridge, is it?"

"You'd think it would be encouraged, at least the walking part. Definitely better than drinking and *driving* onto a bridge."

"Now I'm wondering how many drinks I had," said Jack. "Let me figure this out. Let's say seven bars times one-and-a-half drinks. Ten and a half? Hmm . . . doesn't seem like enough."

Aria giggled. "Enough for what?"

Deputy Lane was no longer banging on the window, having joined
Sam after she convinced him to leave Jack and Aria a few more
minutes to warm up. She was now holding court with Lane and the
other public servants.

"If they're drunk," she said, "they'll still be drunk two minutes
from now."

The four of them gathered at the rear of the ambulance, its doors
open, and Sam decided it was time to discuss what to do with their
new patients.

"I think it's important to check them out as soon as possible. Connor actually recognizes the girl from earlier. He says she took a pretty
good spill off a street corner, and he was the one who put those
butterfly stitches in her forehead." She paused. "By the way, nice
work on those, Connor. Amazing that they stayed on in the river."

Sam turned her attention back to the group.

"I'm thinking there's a good chance they're in shock. I mean, they
fished themselves out of the water, right? Did they say anything
before we got here, like how they ended up in the river in the first
place?"

She directed the question to Sergeant Thompson, correctly assuming he was first on the scene.

"No, as a matter of fact they haven't. Other than their first names,
I don't think they've said much of anything since we all got here."

Deputy Lane spoke up.

"Maybe you're right, Sam. Maybe they're in shock, but I think we
need some answers, don't you? I mean, we've got two people who, as
far as we can tell, decided this was a good time to go night swimming.
I think we need to find out why."

Sergeant Thompson nodded in agreement.

"He's right. They should be warm enough by now, so you two can give them a once over."

Lane was struck with an idea.

"They could be smuggling something, you know?"

Sergeant Thompson started to shake with laughter.

"These two? Oh, God no. Let's see—smuggling from Kentucky to Ohio, via swimming the river on a dark winter night? Nothing wrong with *that* picture." He rolled his eyes. "But I do want to get some questions answered."

Jack and Aria were warmer than they'd been since before they went off the bridge. They sat in the back of the cruiser working on their story while they had the opportunity.

"Okay, Jack. Agreed. We avoid that whole topic, give them the romantic date story, and see if they fall for it."

Jack nodded, suppressing a laugh at Aria referring to their time together as a romantic date.

Aria was sure they could pull off the lie about *why* they were on the bridge, figuring they could actually tell the truth about the *way* they ended up in the river. Or at least most of the truth. When telling a lie, she knew, it was best to retain as much truth as possible, and the true story had the additional benefit of making Jack look the hero which, in Aria's estimation, he really was, though Jack was thinking the same of her.

Of course, that same truth made *her* look like a klutz, but she was willing to accept the potential embarrassment if it meant they would get through the rest of their "date" with as few complications as possible.

Jack broke into her train of thought. "Fingers crossed. But I think we need to work on our lie a little more. I just don't think they're going to fall for it. Are two people, on a date, really going to *walk* across a bridge in a snowstorm?"

"Think about it, Jack. Two people in their twenties, hot for each other, convince themselves it would be romantic to walk across a snowy, iconic bridge at night. I mean, it may not be Romeo and Juliet, but it definitely sounds believable."

Aria smiled at him from her side of the car.

Jack realized Aria didn't know he was actually thirty, but decided now was not the time to correct her.

"Okay, Juliet. I suppose you're right. Let's use the 'young lovers' story and do our best to sell it."

"Young lovers? Is that what we're calling ourselves?"

"Oh yeah, all we need is a balcony and a couple of sonnets."

By then, the temperature in the car was high enough to allow Jack and Aria to shed their wet coats, but they kept the dry blankets over their shoulders. Now, with bodies calm and more comfortable than they'd been in hours, their adrenaline levels declined further.

Having decided on a course of action, they sat silently recounting their story, waiting to learn their fate. The film of moisture—alternately glowing red, white and blue—that covered the interior of the windows prevented them from observing the deliberations taking place at the rear of the ambulance. They dozed, the heat, exhaustion and alcohol leaving them little choice, at least until Deputy Lane's window whacking startled them once again.

Fully awake, Aria grabbed Jack's arm. "Listen, Jack. I can't get arrested again. I just can't." Her panic was more obvious than earlier.

"What? Arrested *again*? What do you mean?"

The beam from Lane's flashlight attempted to pierce the fogged window.

"I don't have time to tell you, Jack. I just need you to know I can't get arrested again."

Lane's voice penetrated the window. "Hey, you two, we need you to come over to the ambulance to get checked out."

Just as the interior window fog made it impossible for Jack and Aria to see much of anything outside the vehicle, it also prevented anyone from seeing in, so Deputy Lane could only assume the occupants heard what he'd said. He decided to give them just a moment more before he opened the door.

Jack and Aria stared at each other, both surprised by Aria's confession, and neither able to move. They understood Officer Lane's instructions, even with his voice muffled by the glass.

"Well, I guess we should . . ."

"Yeah, let's go ahead and get . . ."

Their exit was hampered by their ignorance. Jack had never been in the back seat of a police car, and Aria was handcuffed during the experience to which she alluded moments before, so neither understood that the rear doors of cop cars are designed to prevent detainees from opening them.

Officer Lane heard them try the handle a few times before he heard a muted voice from the back seat.

"Excuse me, sir?"

It was the man's voice.

"We can't open the door."

Without saying a word, Lane pulled the door open and as it swung wide Jack and Aria, who'd piled against it in their futile attempt to get it open, spilled out of the back seat and onto the snowy pavement, reenacting their clump-in-the-snow routine, an image not lost on Sergeant Thompson, observing the scene from a few yards away.

*Still, not an alligator.*

"Sorry about that. I didn't think you'd be right against the door" Officer Lane apologized to the fallen bodies and offered them his hand. "Let's get the two of you over to the ambulance."

Once recovered and back on their feet, Jack and Aria followed Officer Lane to the ambulance, where Sam and Connor waited patiently.

The temperature difference between the interior of the cruiser and the outside world struck Jack and Aria, who were now coatless and had failed to grab their new blankets from the back seat of the sheriff's car. But Sam came to the rescue, producing two more blankets from the ambulance.

Sergeant Thompson had been waiting also.

"Well, I imagine you two have quite a story to tell, so let's see if we can't kill two birds with one stone. If you don't mind, I'll have the paramedics here make sure there's not too much damage to your bodies, and I'll just ask you a few questions. Okay?"

Thompson stared at Aria's forehead as he spoke, only pretending to ask permission for the questioning which was, as all were well aware, a foregone conclusion.

Jack and Aria responded, almost simultaneously.

"Um...yessir."

"Well then, let's get this show on the road. I'm not sure you two lovers noticed, but it's snowing pretty hard out here, so we're going to keep things moving."

Jack and Aria, unprepared for the officer's pithy assessment of their relationship status, tried to deny his appraisal, temporarily forgetting their carefully concocted lie.

"Oh, well, we're not really a couple," said Aria. "You know, it was just . . ."

"Yeah, she's right, officer. It was just a random, like, 'Oh, what a funny thing to run into you tonight' kind of thing. I mean, I wasn't even sure I'd see her tonight."

Jack looked down at Aria who, now remembering the plan, returned his glance with a terse smile.

"Yes, we *did* know we'd see each other, Jack. We were on a *date*." Her voice was tense. "We just didn't set a time, at least not at first."

Sergeant Thompson was pleased his charges could actually speak though he was not terribly interested in what they were saying.

Lane, however, suspected perhaps they were not only drunk but lying for some nefarious reason, one he had yet to fathom. "So was it a date, or wasn't it?"

Sergeant Thompson raised his hand to silence the young officer. "I've got this, Tommie." He looked back at Jack and Aria.

"Well, alrighty then." He glanced at his watch. "Look, I'll be honest with you two. I don't care if you just started dating ten minutes ago. You can go ahead and post that on the Facebook. What I would like to know, for starters, is your last name."

He looked first at Jack.

"Current."

"Yes, your current last name."

"It's Current. My last name is Current."

"So, you're Jack Current. Well, that's a little tricky, isn't it?"

Sergeant Thompson scribbled Jack's name in his notebook, an object Jack had begun to covet. He wanted to ask the Sergeant if he had a spare, but thought better of it. The situation was already weird enough.

"And what about you, young lady? Can I get your name, please?"

Aria hesitated. "It's Aria. Aria Balfour."

Sergeant Thompson scribbled while a small wave of embarrassment washed over Jack. He had not known Aria's last name until that moment.

*Did I need to jump off a bridge to learn her last name?*

Sergeant Thompson went about the business of gathering pertinent personal information from the two people who he, in his mind, started calling "river rats" because it flowed better than "river lungfish." He was practiced and methodical in his inquiry, even though he knew the paramedics were waiting, hiding from the wind in the back of the ambulance. The conditions were less than optimal, but he had a job to do.

"And just how did you two end up in the river?"

This was the question for which Jack and Aria prepared, and once they started, the info came fast and furious. Thompson did his best to keep up with his notes.

Jack got the ball rolling. "See, we were on a date, up in OTR. You know, the date we agreed on."

Aria jumped in. "Right, and so we were just going to have a couple drinks."

"And then the snow started getting heavy . . ."

"And we thought it would be cool to take a walk in it."

"And then, without really thinking about it, we ended up . . ."

"On the bridge, which was icy, and then . . ."

"Well, yeah, she slipped on a patch of ice and went over the rail."

"And then Jack jumped in after me."

"And, I guess, you know. Here we are now."

As they poured out their story, Lane directed his scowl at whichever miscreant was speaking, head on a swivel, hoping one or both of them would slip up or crack completely.

Thompson, on the other hand, was doing his best to keep up with the chatter and faithfully record it in his notebook, despite the falling snow, which melted on the pages and smeared some of the ink. His note-taking was interrupted by one of the EMTs.

"Sarge, you guys going to be done with them soon? We're getting cold."

Connor was anxious to move the process along. He and Samantha had already decided to take Jack and Aria to the hospital, though neither had yet to say anything that sounded an alarm bell from a medical perspective. But even though the couple appeared to be of sound body, minus the treatable cuts and bruises, the medics knew the river was teeming with items on which they could have bonked their heads. They were on the lookout for tell-tale signs of a concussion.

Officer Lane spoke up.

"Just one more thing and they're all yours."

Sergeant Thompson knew what Lane was thinking.

"Tommie, I don't think we're going to be able to do a sobriety test. It's too slippery out here."

Officer Lane shrugged in silent protest while Jack and Aria breathed sighs of relief. Neither had any confidence they could walk a straight line, or even see a straight line. But Lane had not given up.

## Chapter Four

## Tased and Confused

When it came to procedure, Deputy Lane was a master, and decided he wasn't going to defer to the more experienced Thompson. His training informed him that, in a situation such as this, it was imperative to determine whether or not the "suspects" were under the influence.

"Sarge, a word please?"

Thompson and Lane stepped aside for a private conversation. Jack and Aria watched anxiously, hoping the older officer would win the day, but expecting the opposite. After all, if either of them was in the same position as the cops, they would certainly do their best to determine if the morons in question were under the influence. While the two deputies discussed the fine points of impairment according to the Hamilton County Sheriff's policy manual, Jack took the opportunity to speak to Aria.

"How bad could it be?"

Aria pulled her blanket tighter around her shoulders. "Well, I'm not sure. Have you ever been drunk tested before?"

"Oh, sure. Hundreds of times." Jack rolled his eyes. "Just kidding. You?"

Aria hesitated. "Well, just the once. But mostly I've only seen it on TV, where everyone looks ridiculous, even if they pass."

Jack hesitated. "Do you want to tell me about the one time you got drunk tested?"

Aria tried to whisper through wind. "I can't right now, but it's part of why . . . why I can't get arrested again."

Jack was startled. There was that word, the one from the cop car: "again." He wanted to pursue its meaning but Aria spoke first.

"How drunk are you."

Jack abandoned further questions about Aria's *first* drunk test and gave himself a once-over.

"Depends on who you ask."

"You. I'm asking you." She almost added "dumbass" but managed to edit herself. Aria felt impatient. She didn't know how long they had until the deputies finished their confab.

"Okay. Well, I guess, drunker than I was ten minutes ago, but not as drunk as I was on the bridge."

"Okay, that's good. I think. And, you know, so what if we don't pass? It's not like we were driving a car, or even a scooter. For God's sake, all we were doing was walking across a bridge. Well...sort of...okay, not necessarily walking. More like falling." Aria sounded more hopeful than she felt.

"We definitely walked on the bridge, you know, before the falling."

"Sure. Something like that."

Aria's brain replayed the scene of the two of them on the bridge.

*Did I fall? Did I jump? Does it matter?*

She pushed the questions out of her head. She was sure, or nearly sure, she didn't jump and, if she *did* jump, that the act was subconscious. If she did jump, she had more to worry about than she thought. But this was not the time to deal with potential demons. She could do that later, after she dealt with her current ones, *after* they passed the drunk test. Or not.

Jack interrupted her internal dialogue.

"Okay, so how drunk are *you*?"

"Hmm. Not too bad, I think." Aria paused. "But we'll see. When I was, you know, searching for you, I grabbed a couple drinks along the way."

Jack smiled. "A couple?"

Aria attempted to cipher her level of consumption and took a wild guess.

"Maybe more than a couple, but still in the single digits. High single digits, maybe?" She was sure she was undercounting.

Their conversation was interrupted by the deputies, whose demeanor indicated Lane won the argument.

Sergeant Thompson spoke first.

"Well, Jack and Aria, just so you know, Deputy Lane was kind enough to remind me that it's illegal to jump off any of these here bridges." Thompson waved his hand toward the river, where the lights of three or four bridges were visible, even in the snowstorm. "Because of that, we determined that we need to verify your sobriety, or lack thereof. Do either of you have any objections?"

Thompson looked hopeful, as if he *wanted* one or both of them to object. They did not. Unbeknownst to them, they actually could have said no, but their lack of experience in the arena of sobriety testing, and law enforcement in general, crippled their judgment. So, instead of rejecting the test, they nodded like bobblehead dolls, intent on being cooperative so as not to arouse any further suspicion.

*Why is he asking? Why isn't he just barking orders at us?*

In addition to doubts they harbored about their own blood alcohol levels, it was now apparent to Jack and Aria there was a chance they actually could get pinched for breaking a law. It hadn't occurred to either of them that jumping off a bridge was illegal. Now, however, the need for such a law suddenly seemed painfully obvious.

Aria leaned in to whisper to Jack.

"Well, damn, why *wouldn't* it be illegal to jump off a bridge?"

Jack shrugged, not sure if he agreed or not. For him, getting arrested was the least of his concerns. Had his evening gone according to plan, he'd be dead already, thereby eliminating the need to explain his behavior to anyone who cared to ask. He had, after all, written the log as a chronicle, an apology, an explanation of why he was going to do what he eventually failed to do.

To Jack's addled brain, that failure was now biting him in the ass. That failure now made it necessary to make up a story about what happened on the bridge, or what didn't happen on the bridge, depending on how you looked at it, and risk any consequences that might accompany the truth. Standing next to Aria, he told himself it was better to stick to the lie they'd concocted, and keep sticking to it, until everyone, including themselves, believed it.

*Wait.*

"Aria," Jack kept his voice as low as possible. "What about the log?"

Aria shrugged. "I don't think now's a good time to look for it, Jack."

Jack spoke through clenched teeth, trying not to move his lips. "But it has everything in it. Everything. It explains what I, what we, were doing on the bridge."

"That's bad. That's bad." Aria now understood. "What if they find it?"

"Exactly."

"We have to find it before they do."

"Yes. That would be optimal. Any ideas?"

"No, but I'll let you know if I come up with anything *before* they handcuff us."

As Sergeant Thompson wrote some notes, the wail of another siren broke everyone's concentration. A red firetruck pulled alongside the other vehicles and emptied four firefighters onto the pavement of the parking lot.

Jack and Aria were now outnumbered four to one, further diminishing any chance of escape if they still held such a hope. She tried to smile at him.

"Is this what it means when they say the cavalry is coming?"

"Jeez. There are so many uniforms."

One of the firemen, whose name was Donald, approached Sam.

"Sorry, we're a little late," he said. "The snow's got everything going crazy."

"Tell me about it." Sam pointed in the direction of Jack and Aria. "We're still trying to get these two into the rig and get 'em out of here."

"What's the holdup?"

Sam pointed at the sheriffs.

"Ask them."

Donald walked over to Deputy Lane, who was now scribbling in *his* notebook, and struck up a conversation.

"Good evening, Deputy. Can you bring me up to speed?"

Lane did not appreciate the distraction. He knew the firetruck was there because the policy manual said it had to be, but at this point he felt the extra uniforms were just a pain in the ass. For him, their presence served no purpose other than to interrupt his "investigation." Had he the authority, he would have sent them away.

"Nothing much going on now." Deputy Lane furrowed his brow and waved his pen toward Jack and Aria, barely looking up from his note-taking. "We got a call about these two crawling out of the river a while ago and we're trying to figure out the whys and wherefores."

Fireman Donald realized there was no chance of getting out of there until the deputy had his way with the two people wrapped in blankets.

"Alright, Deputy, let me know if we can be of any assistance."

Lane gave the firefighter a cursory nod and went back to his notebook. Once finished, he slipped the notebook in his pocket and turned to Sergeant Thompson.

"You ready to go?"

"It's your show, Tommie."

"Then, ladies first, I guess."

Deputy Lane walked to Aria.

"Miss, please hand the blanket to the paramedic and step over here with me."

As if in a daze, Aria removed the blanket and handed it to Sam. Her clothes had managed to dry out a little in the police cruiser, but she was no longer wearing the stadium jacket her friend Tracy had given her earlier that evening. It was still in Thompson's cruiser. The freezing wind tore through her thin top and Aria now regretted her work-appropriate clothing choice, longing for something more substantial.

Deputy Lane surveyed the slippery parking lot, the entirety of which was sufficiently level for his purpose. He smiled at Aria as he turned to face her.

"Okay, Miss, since we really can't see the pavement, so I won't ask you to walk a straight line."

Deputy Lane's feeble attempt at a joke fell flat, so he asserted his command of the situation in an attempt to hide his embarrassment.

"Okay, Miss, what I'd like you to do is lift your right knee until your thigh is parallel to the surface of the pavement, and then touch your left index finger to your nose."

Aria was perplexed. Had she been thrust into some bizarre version of a yoga class? What did lifting her leg and touching her nose have to do with being drunk?

"Huh?"

Lane recognized her confusion and was kind enough to demonstrate. "Like this."

To the surprise of no one, the deputy's demonstration was wildly unsuccessful. Seconds into the attempt, Lane found himself frantically sliding forward and, falling with a grunt, hysterically splaying himself on the ground as if attempting a belly-down snow angel. Aria suppressed a giggle while Jack blurted a short laugh, doing his best to transmute the laugh into a cough.

Caught off-guard by the level of Lane's disaster, the rest of the "team" froze. The firefighters looked at each other, waiting to see who would be first to render assistance. But Aria didn't hesitate. Without a word, she grabbed his arm and struggled to help him to his feet. Finally, two of the firefighters joined her to help.

Aria, still shivering, found the whole situation ludicrous.

*Why are we doing this? Don't they have breathalyzers in their cars?*

She stopped herself from asking this out loud, figuring a breathalyzer might actually be a bad idea, and that it made sense to give their bodies as much time as possible to process the copious amounts of alcohol they'd ingested. So, she remained silent, checked her balance, and looked to Deputy Lane for further instructions. His demeanor was embarrassed but determined.

"Your turn. Good luck." He almost sounded like he meant it.

Aria nodded, tried not to panic and did her best to emulate the movement Lane intended but, like Lane, disaster struck immediately. As Aria began to lift her knee, her body was wracked by a violent shiver. The jolt threw her off balance, her spastic attempt to stay vertical eliciting a collective gasp from the burgeoning crowd of uniforms formed into a semi-circle around the flailing Aria. Connor and Sam, still worried about the possibility of a concussion, rushed in to steady her.

Sam gave Deputy Lane a withering look. "How about we avoid any more head trauma tonight?"

Sergeant Thompson spoke diplomatically. "You know, Deputy Lane, considering the conditions, we may have to forego the physical test."

Lane nodded. Despite the young sheriff's keen desire to follow procedure, his own fall and the girl's tumble spooked him. He had no desire to expose anyone to injury, including himself, or to complete the requisite paperwork for said injuries.

"I agree, Sarge. We can always check their blood alcohol levels at the hospital."

Hearing the words "blood alcohol" made Aria anxious and strengthened her desire to avoid being breathalyzed. She needed to be bold.

"No, I'd like to try the test again. I think I can do it."

Watching from his end of the semi-circle, holding her blanket and wrapped in his own, Jack had a sneaking suspicion she was trying to take one for the team—that she believed if they passed a roadside drunk test, that would be the end of it. He wasn't wrong. That was exactly what she was thinking. Aria calculated that the successful accomplishment of the balancing act would shield them from further probing into the evening's drinking. But Jack, impressed by her courage, decided he could not allow her go it alone, and threw himself into the fray.

"I think I can do it, too. I want to try."

All eyes turned to Jack, who had already tossed their blankets into the back of the ambulance. The emergency personnel seemed a bit stunned, but Sergeant Thompson was intrigued. Despite the lack of alligators, the night was finally getting interesting.

Before Sam or Connor could mount a protest, Jack started to move toward Aria, as if he was getting ready to repeat what she had just attempted. But Jack had a plan, hastily conceived, and it was twofold: he would save Aria from certain death or grave injury or, at a minimum, failing a drunk test, whilst simultaneously taking a shot at recovering his precious Drunk Log. He'd started to believe the current might actually have carried it to the eddy behind the barge, to their landing spot on the riverbank.

*Paper floats, at least for a while. Maybe it's close.*

His desire to find the notebook had taken on an increased importance: He needed to keep it out of the hands of the authorities. That desire was growing like a tumor, and was now as overwhelming as his desire *not* to allow Aria to try to save him twice in one evening, first at the bridge, and now in the icy parking lot.

*No, it's my turn to save her...and the Log.*

Those two thoughts drove him and, relieved of the blanket, Jack strode confidently toward Deputy Lane. On the fourth step, however, he flashed a smile at Lane, turned abruptly, and made a hard left toward the river. He then broke into a run, or at least as much of a run as he could muster, still handicapped by stiff muscles and the hip injury he'd suffered a year before. But the run, for reasons he didn't understand, felt glorious. And it *was* glorious. The folks in uniform couldn't believe what was happening, couldn't take their eyes off the crazy man running in the snow toward the river.

Sergeant Thompson shrugged.

*The night just keeps getting more interesting.*

Though the parking lot was treacherous, Jack managed to keep his footing and as the tree line loomed closer, he headed for the spot where he and Aria had emerged. As he picked his way down in the dim light, dodging trees and chunks of broken concrete, he scanned the water's edge for anything notebook-sized, anything notebook-colored. Perhaps it actually *was* caught in the floating pool of debris trapped between the barge and the bank.

Jack was wrong, of course. The notebook was not to be found, not a single page of it, and he would never see it again. But still he searched, stupidly certain he would find it, knowing he had to find it. And he was just as stupidly certain his escape would be enough to stop what was happening to Aria, would be enough to prove he had her back, just as she had his. If he was lucky, he could save her and the Drunk Log all in one fell swoop.

But he was not lucky, and would accomplish only one of those things. Just as Jack had hoped, his escape to the river caused Deputy Lane to lose focus, momentarily forgetting all about the sobriety test he was administering to the girl he suspected of...what? Because when Jack started running, all of Tommie Lane's instincts, as a cop and as a man, screamed at him to run after Jack.

"Hey! Stop!"

The young deputy was yelling at Jack's back as it floated over the snow. But Jack did not do as instructed. He did not stop. And so Tommie Lane ran after him, slipping and sliding across the lot, while the onlookers stared in amazement as the two men, one bedraggled, one still crisply uniformed, disappeared down the embankment.

Jack heard the voice tell him to stop, but had no intention of doing so—at least not until he had pulled all the unwanted attention away from Aria. Not until he found his log. But the distance to the river was surprisingly short and he was forced to stop. Deputy Lane caught up to him seconds after he reached the barge.

"Now, listen Jack, just hold still. We need to get you back up to the lot."

Jack heard Deputy Lane's voice behind him, but still did not respond. Instead, he scanned the riverbank for his prize.

*Is it further downriver?*

The idea plagued him.

*How far could a stupid notebook travel in an hour?*

His engineer's brain went on autopilot, multiplying the average speed of the river's flow by the amount of time he estimated had passed since he and Aria crawled out of the river.

"It could be two miles away by now." Jack spoke out loud, without intending to, as if someone else was collaborating with him on his mathematics. "Or it could be close."

"What? What are you talking about?" Lane was confused.

Jack continued to ignore the deputy who had, unbeknownst to Jack, drawn the taser from his utility belt. Jack's brain had moved on and was now reckoning the length of time it would take him to cover two-plus miles in the snow, wondering if he would be lucky enough to find the notebook if he tried.

*Yes. I have to.*

Staring downriver, Jack plotted his path along the bank for as far as he could see, which wasn't far, and started to move, but before he could take three steps, 50,000 volts streamed into his body, courtesy of Deputy Lane's taser. The electric gun had been deployed with lightning efficiency at the first indication Jack was going rogue, and rendered him immobile.

Post-tasing, Jack's first vision was of two sheriff's hats hovering over him, floating and unattached to anything solid. He was flat on his back, with no recollection of how he got there. Within seconds, however, his memory returned. The taser didn't hurt so much as feel like a large, uncontrollable charley horse encompassing his entire body. It was not a pleasant experience.

"Alright, son, let's get you up on your feet."

Jack recognized the voice of Sergeant Thompson. Without asking permission, he and Deputy Lane each slipped a hand under one of Jack's shoulders and brought him to an upright position. Given the intensity of the voltage, the cramp was wearing off more quickly than Jack expected. Before he knew it, he was being pushed and pulled up the treacherous embankment by the two officers while light from handheld torches streamed toward them from above. Once they reached the top and emerged from the tree line, he could see the firefighters' faces. He could see Aria just behind, held in place by two paramedics, looks of concern and admiration fighting for control of her face.

His plan had worked, or at least the distraction part worked. No one, except the paramedics, was even looking at Aria. Had it not been for them, she could have easily slipped away, unnoticed.

Jack's plan to locate the Drunk Log on a riverbank—at night in a snowstorm—turned out to be a bit of a shipwreck, a result he should have been able to predict with little effort. He was, after all, an engineer, a person whose brain was guided by logic and proven outcomes. But in that unexpected moment his brain set aside all its training, all its experience, and told him to go for it, told him to go find his damn notebook, come hell or high water. The fact the odds of success were miniscule didn't hold him back, and for his trouble he was knocked unconscious by a standard tool of law enforcement.

Jack figured something else. Something good. He realized there was no way anyone was ever going to find the notebook. It was likely already too far downriver and no one in authority would even know to look for it. So, while part of him would have loved to recover the pad, another part, the part that wanted to keep his secrets, felt satisfied that his written words would not be used against him in a court of law. The tasing was a small price to pay for all he had accomplished during his short getaway attempt.

Deputy Lane, however, was not as thrilled. "You know, the worst thing you can do is run."

Deputy Thompson heard the comment, and nodded in agreement. But by now they were back with the "team," and Thompson, despite their entertainment value, was more than ready to hand the miscreants over to the paramedics, write up the report, and finish his shift, minus any alligators. Or lungfish. Deputy Lane, on the other hand, was still coursing with adrenaline. It had been weeks since he'd tased anyone.

"And another thing, asshole, don't try that again."

Jack heard the words, and so did everyone else, including Aria.

Donald the fireman had had enough. "Listen, Deputy, I don't want to tell you how to do your job, but haven't these two been through enough tonight? Do you really have to be such a dick?"

Deputy Lane, though startled by the comment, was not one to back down.

*Who does this fireman think he is?*

"I'll tell you what. You don't tell me how to do my job and I won't tell you how to do yours. Cool?"

Sergeant Thompson, who happened to share Fireman Donald's viewpoint in this particular situation, was nevertheless ready to jump in on the side of his fellow deputy, but Samantha beat him to the punch.

"He's right, Deputy. We need to get these two to the hospital. They've been out here for way too long already, and if anything happens to them because you two made them stand around in the snow in wet clothes, I'll testify for *them*."

Deputy Lane felt outnumbered.

"You know what? *He* ran from *me*. I was just following procedure."

The last comment garnered a group protest from everyone except the fugitives and Sergeant Thompson. Angry words flew fast and furious, and though Deputy Lane knew it was time to retreat, he took time to fire one last shot.

"Fine. You all take them with you, but I want a blood alcohol level on both of them once you get them to the hospital. And I'm going to put it in my report, along with how uncooperative you all have been."

Lane turned back to his car, slipped on the ice, recovered as fast as he could and snapped at the rest of his colleagues, some of whom were suppressing smiles.

"And one more thing. I'll be coming by the hospital to check on this, so no games!"

Finally, Jack and Aria were led to the ambulance, surrounded by a protective knot of firefighters and paramedics. Aria was determined to question Jack on his judgment, but wouldn't have the opportunity until they were alone, an opportunity she was not sure would present itself any time soon. Still, she'd found it exhilarating to watch him run back to the river, suspecting he was doing it for her, just as she had taken the drunk test for him.

Loaded into the back of the ambulance and again wrapped in the warm blankets, Jack and Aria sat facing each other from opposite sides of the rig. The paramedics went about the business of checking on the physical well-being of their new patients as the truck bounced its way toward the hospital. Now, with a moment to rest and think, a thought dawned on Aria. The thought brought a smile to her face.

*I saved Jack.*

Jack, his eyes locked on hers, was lost in his own thoughts.

*I saved Aria.*

# Chapter Five

## Night of the Rig

Safe and secure in the back of the vehicle the paramedics kept calling "the rig," Jack and Aria began to doze again. The hard seats of the rig weren't nearly as comfortable as the back seat of Sergeant Thompson's police car, but sleep was chasing them, even as they bounced along in the back of a glorified truck. Given the late hour and the numerous infusions of alcohol they'd consumed earlier, combined with the near constant waxing and waning of adrenaline, it was no surprise Jack and Aria were having trouble mustering the will to fend off sleep. Only the bumps and shimmies of the ambulance kept them awake, that and the consistent stream of questions and chatter emanating from Sam and Connor.

The driver, who had opted to remain in the rig and play Sudoku on his phone during the entire escapade by the river, hit the brakes to avoid a vehicle skidding in front of them. The sudden stop nearly threw Jack and Aria from their benches, but they were held in place by Connor and Sam.

"You guys okay back there?"

Sam gave the driver a thumbs up through the small opening separating the front of the truck from the back and returned their attention back to their passengers.

"Take it slow," Connor said. "The roads are terrible."

"Let's get there in one piece," said Sam.

"Roger that." The disembodied voice of the driver drifted back to them.

Sam and Connor decided to divide and conquer, each choosing a "victim" on whom they could focus their efforts. In this case, each chose the patient of the opposite sex and, as soon as the back doors were closed and the ambulance moving, went efficiently about their business to determine the extent and nature of their passenger's injuries.

"Do you remember hitting your head on anything?"

"Do you mind if I pull your sleeve up?"

"I'm going to take your blood pressure now."

"Where do you have the most pain?"

Attacking the situation two-on-two, Samantha and Connor calmly went about their respective examinations whilst simultaneously fielding the occasional radio-dispatch inquiry from whichever emergency room they were headed.

"Do you remember me from earlier?" Connor was examining the butterfly stitches he had placed on her forehead several hours earlier, when Aria had taken a tumble off a curb and conked her head on the street.

To her chagrin, Aria hadn't recognized Connor until that moment. "Yeah, yeah, okay, yeah. Now I do. Wow. You sure get around, don't you?"

Connor laughed. "I suppose I do, especially on a double shift, but Cincinnati's not super-big, you know?"

Aria nodded.

"It's really not," Sam chimed in from her side of the rig.

"I guess I'm not that memorable," Connor said.

"Well, don't take it too hard. Remember, I might have a concussion or two."

Connor laughed again. "Oddly enough, that makes me feel better."

Exhausted and in a fog, Jack heard the flirtatious conversation between his would-be girlfriend and the man tending to her physical well-being. He was curious as to the circumstances of her curb fall but didn't take the opportunity to ask. That would have required a succession of words *and* the ability to listen carefully to the answer, both of which seemed beyond his reach at the moment. Besides the eavesdropping, Jack's brain was busy recalling the miserable failure that defined the second part of his "distract and search" plan. Sure, while he could confidently claim the first part was wildly successful at saving Aria from the sobriety test, it all ended poorly when it came to retrieving the notebook, even though its permanent disappearance had some positive benefits.

There was paper all around him, he noted silently, and wondered if they would let him have some, wondered if it would be okay to start a brand-new log. He wondered if they'd give him a pen. When he had a moment, during which Sam was taking his blood pressure and not asking questions, he looked across the three feet of space separating him from Aria. She saw him, too, and smiled while he pantomimed a writing motion with his free hand. Despite her own exhaustion, and feeling sick to her stomach from the bouncing truck, Aria understood what Jack was trying to tell her.

"Connor, can I ask you a favor?" Aria gave him a little smile.

She was aware that men tended to find her attractive, and rarely did she consciously use this to her advantage, but at the moment she was determined to use her wiles to get Jack what he wanted and needed.

"Could Jack borrow a pen and some paper? He just needs to write something down before he forgets it." Aria was as coy as possible considering she had dried mud in her hair.

Connor McCleod was surprised. "You know, I've never ever had a customer ask me for something to write on."

"I'm sure that's true." Aria continued her attempt to obtain paper and a writing instrument for Jack. "It would be weird if everyone in the back of an ambulance asked you for pen and paper, wouldn't it?"

The paramedics giggled.

*Yes, it would be weird if our patients all wanted to write stuff while they rode in the rig.*

"Funny, right?" Aria pressed. "But, you know, I'm kinda serious. We've had a really long night and we just need to do this thing, so please, can you help?"

Neither paramedic made a move to follow through on the request, but when Connor started to chuckle again, Sam interrupted.

"Just get him some damn paper, Connor. And a pen."

Connor, startled into action by the sharpness of Sam's command, put down his stethoscope and started looking around for something on which Jack could write. There was nothing readily available, as the only paper on hand were blank medical forms clamped onto clipboards, hanging from hooks.

Connor, having completed a visual search of his immediate surroundings, confronted Aria with the results.

"There's no paper, except for these forms." He held one of them up to prove he wasn't lying.

"What about the driver?" Aria wasn't going to stop until she got what she wanted. "Would he have anything up there?"

"Oh, right. Good thinking."

Connor swiveled on his seat and spoke through the small, windowless hole separating him from the driver. "Hey man, you got any notebooks or paper up there? We need some back here."

As luck would have it, the driver had a stack of small, cop-sized notebooks stacked on the passenger seat next to him. He had picked them up earlier to hand out to his fellow paramedics, all of whom, he'd determined on a previous shift, could benefit from having something to write on.

He grabbed one from the stack and handed it back through the hole, never taking his eyes off the road.

"Thanks, dude."

Connor held the notebook triumphantly aloft, attempting to impress his new friend Aria, who was in the process of removing a twig from her hair.

"Look what I've got."

"That's fantastic, Connor. Do you mind giving it to Jack? Along with a pen?"

Though disappointed Aria wasn't more dazzled by his resourcefulness, Connor did as he was asked.

Jack watched the scene unfold with interest. He could have asked for a pen and paper as easily as she, he knew, but it was more fun to watch her take control. Rumpled, beaten up and exhausted, Aria still had her wits about her, and while she led Connor where she needed him to go, Jack told himself he would find a way to pay her back for everything she had done for him that evening.

Getting tased on her behalf was a good start, perhaps, but it wasn't enough. He felt he would have to get tased at least five more times to make himself worthy of everything she had done for him thus far.

Jack took the notebook from Connor's hand, and a pen from Sam, who had a spare and wanted to contribute to whatever was happening. He gave them a nod of thanks and then bowed his head, staring at the inside of the tiny notebook.

His first thought about writing in the diminutive pad was that he would have to write really small. His second thought was that the events of the last couple hours had actually given him too much to write about, that he had no idea how he would fit all of it in a three-by-five-inch booklet containing, maybe, twenty sheets of paper.

*Considering everything else, this is a small problem.*

He began to write, as the ambulance slowly bounced over Cincinnati's slippery streets.

*2:16 AM*

*There's a clock in this ambulance,*
*It's late, or early, depending on your point of view.*
*I'm here with Aria. She's sitting right across from me.*
*She's talking to the ambulance guy and I'm thankful she's here.*
*It's been the craziest night of my life, and for some reason I can't*
*imagine having spent it with anyone else.*
*Is this love? Is this what love is? What it feels like?*
*I don't know. I think I'm still drunk, or it could be the tasing.*
*I don't remember everything that led me here.*
*I know almost nothing about what led her here.*
*She's looking at me...Aria, I mean.*
*She's looking at me from the other side of the ambulance while I*
*write in this notebook, the one she got for me.*
*She's smiling.*
*I wonder what I can do for her. I owe her everything.*

"What are you writing?"

Sam was watching Jack write. It was an innocent question. She couldn't know how annoying he might find it.

"Oh, you know, just trying to catch up with all of this." He waved his arm expansively, a motion meant to encompass more than just the receiving end of the ambulance.

Jack was afraid to be honest with Sam, afraid if he was honest with her that nothing would be secret, that she likely had sworn some sort of solemn oath promising never to hide what her patients told her while they were riding in the rig. He tried to look in her eyes, tried to discern the motives behind her question, and concluded he was being paranoid. Her eyes held nothing sinister or dishonest, and Jack decided she was just making conversation, like a dozen others from the night before.

"Well, whatever it is, that's yours to keep. But you might want to slow it down a little." Sam pointed at the notebook. "There aren't a lot of pages there. Matter of fact . . ."

Sam turned her attention from Jack and called to the driver through the small opening.

"Hey! Can we get another one of those notebooks?"

The driver grunted, reached across to the passenger seat, grabbed another notebook from the shrink-wrapped stack and threaded it back through the hole to Sam, who passed it on to Jack.

"Here you go. You can save this one for later."

Jack was moved by Sam's kindness, more than he understood, and within seconds of gingerly taking the blank notebook from her hand, found himself doing something he hadn't done in a year. He cried.

At first, Jack held back the tears, or at least tried to hold them back. In this instance, as in the last one—in the aftermath of the accident that killed his nephew—he wasn't particularly successful. A couple of drops fell from his bowed head and soaked into the open notebook in his lap, blurring the ink. Jack felt ashamed.

*Why am I crying?*

Was his desire to cry a result of this unexpected kindness, a culmination of all the events of the evening, or simple exhaustion? He couldn't be sure and assumed it was likely a combination of all three. He hadn't slept in nearly twenty hours and, of course, there was the whole failed suicide thing, and all the baggage he'd carried to the bridge in the first place.

*Troy. It's been a year since I killed my nephew.*

Aria bore witness to what was happening to Jack from three feet away. She watched the tears well in his eyes after Sam gave him the notebook. Within moments, his tears became hers, and she wanted nothing more than to hold him, to let him know she understood, and so that is what she did. She reached across the empty space between them and wrapped her arms around him. He reached for her in return, allowing himself to sink into the embrace.

Sam and Connor occupied themselves as best they could, not wanting to interrupt such a moment. It certainly wasn't the first time tears had been shed in front of them, and they gave Jack and Aria as much space as was possible in the back of the cramped ambulance, using the time to finish noting the important parts of their respective examinations and to call in their findings to the emergency room.

Sam broke into the moment after Jack and Aria regained their composure.

"Under normal circumstances, we would already be close to the hospital." It was a mindless comment, just something to break the tension.

She waited for a response from either and, receiving none, continued.

"The snow is really slowing us down. It might be another ten minutes or so before we get there."

Theirs was not the only ambulance getting bogged down in the foul weather. Emergency vehicles all over the city were being delayed by the snow and the sheer number of calls received. The snow was unexpected, leaving drivers and road crews unprepared. Cars were sliding into each other all over town. Cincinnati does not lack for hills, and on those hills no parked car, telephone pole, or road sign was immune to poorly controlled automobiles straying off course on icy streets.

Jack and Aria heard Sam talking to them but paid little attention. Tears under control, they had retreated from one another, though their eyes remained locked as they slipped back into the fog of emotional and physical exhaustion, the haze of alcohol still hovering over them.

They were aware of the siren, aware of Sam and Connor, aware of the bumps in the road and the fact they were moving very slowly.

One of the potholes, a particularly wretched one, jolted Jack upright. He had an idea.

"Here, Aria. I want you to have this one." Jack held out the second notebook Sam had acquired for him.

Aria looked at the notebook extending toward her from Jack's hand. "No, Jack. I want you to have it. You can keep the log going."

"I've got one. If I have to, I'll find something else to write in later. But I want you to have this, you know, in case you get the urge. After tonight, we've both got a lot to write about, don't you think?"

Aria took the notebook and held it in her hand. She understood why Jack wanted her to have it but she wasn't ready to write in it. She had never kept a journal for herself, even as a teenager. She held the notebook on her lap, afraid to put it in her damp coat pocket. But it felt good in her hand, and she decided she would put some words in it later, when she had a moment alone.

The driver's voice interrupted her thoughts.

"We've got another pick up."

"What are you talking about?" Connor's face twisted with the question. He and Sam had been working their shift for more than eleven hours and were ready to go home. "This isn't a school bus."

The driver explained from the front seat. "Everybody is running out of rigs because of the weather so they're doubling up when they can."

"Well, damn. Can this night get any weirder?" Connor was asking Sam, who declined to respond, correctly believing the question to be rhetorical. "Who are we picking up? And is it on the way?"

"Yup. It's on the way," The voice of the driver meandered through the hole. "Another drunk, I guess. Wrecked his car and the cops want him at the hospital to take a blood-alcohol. Shouldn't take long."

Given how slow they were going, Connor felt the driver was over-confident in his time assessment. He shook his head in disbelief.

"You two heard that, right?" Sam spoke directly to Jack and Aria. "We're not sure what we're getting ourselves into, so just try to stay out of the way."

Jack and Aria acknowledged Sam's order with affirmative nods. The idea of picking up another passenger perked them up and, in an odd way, gave them something to look forward to. Perhaps the addition of a new person, especially a drunk, might lighten the atmosphere.

Though they hadn't discussed it, as they sat on the benches of the ambulance Jack and Aria started to believe, as had Connor, that the evening could definitely get weirder, that the guardrails they'd built around their lives had dissolved into the ether, leaving the possibilities wide open.

Jack reached across to Aria and took her hand, the one without the notebook in it, and gave it a quick squeeze. He felt punch drunk, or at least how he believed being punch drunk would feel, and found himself strangely anxious to meet the new rider, their new (allegedly) drunken compatriot. The prospect of a new addition to their little ambulance party was oddly exhilarating.

Jack quipped. "Will the lady or gentleman in question be dressed for an evening out?"

Aria smiled and joined in. Jack's burst of energy was infectious.

"Injured or just looking for a free ride to the hospital?"

Jack laughed.

"Boisterous or sullen?"

Jack smiled and shrugged, silently hoping for boisterous.

While her questions bounced around the ambulance, Aria had already moved on, wondering how much more time they would have to spend in the ambulance. Though it was warm enough, she was uncomfortable, crammed into the back of a noisy, bouncy steel box, afraid she may soon relieve herself of the contents of her stomach.

Relief came in the form of their new passenger, for whom the ambulance jolted to a stop. Once stationary, all stared in anticipation at the rear doors, wondering what manner of human would be revealed by their opening.

"Dun dun dun duh . . ." Aria finished the dramatic flourish just as the back doors swung open, giving them full view of their new, fellow traveler.

A Catholic Priest.

The paramedics were only somewhat less surprised than Jack and Aria. The dispatcher had warned the driver that the profession and appearance of the new passenger might catch them off guard, but refused to provide any more information, saying they would understand everything when they'd arrived at the scene.

Sam and Connor were anxious, and as the doors swung open they revealed, sandwiched between two police officers, an inebriated Man of God. The priest looked up as Sam and Connor jumped out to collect him and smiled as they made landfall.

"Well, now," he said. "I suppose you two are here for me."

Neither had ever transported a drunken priest, and while they understood priests to be as human as anyone, the fact he was adorned in cassock and collar threw them. But the arrival of the priest had created another problem: the back of the rig was now over capacity, meaning either Connor or Sam would have to ride in the cab with the driver and his bag of notebooks. Solving such conflicts involved a frantic game of Rock-Paper-Scissors and Sam won the round, defeating Connor's scissors with her rock, and thereby relegating him to the front seat.

Father Randall O'Neal was polite and clearly in good spirits, despite having slid his car into a telephone pole and, in the process, gashing his head on the steering wheel. The priest, however, was feeling no pain, having enjoyed quite a bit of wine earlier that evening.

"We'll take him from here."

Sam and Connor relieved the officers of their guest, each placing one of Father Randall's arms over their shoulders and helping him into the ambulance.

"Ah now, what kind, young people you are."

Though Father Randall had left Ireland as a child, he still retained a tinge of the accent. Sam found it delightful, and was looking forward to making him talk for the remainder of their journey to the hospital.

For their part, Jack and Aria did as they were told, doing their best to stay out of the way of the paramedics and the new passenger, who was a sight to behold—tall and dignified, yet drunk and bloody.

"Well, it seems I've infringed on your ambulance ride, young lady and gentleman. I hope you don't mind if an old priest travels with you for a few minutes."

"No, of course not, Father." Jack managed to speak before Aria. "It should be nice."

Jack immediately regretted his second comment.

*What does that even mean? Why would I say that? 'It should be nice?'*

Jack's self-flagellation aside, Father Randall didn't seem to take notice of the awkward comment, or at least pretended not to. In his years in the priesthood, he had grown used to hearing clumsy things emerge from peoples' mouths.

Aria said nothing. She wasn't sure what she was supposed to say, so she nodded and waved. Father Randall smiled and waved back before turning his attention to Sam, who was busy cleaning the cut on his forehead and sponging the blood trickling down his nose.

# Chapter Six

## A Priest, a Bartender, and
## an Engineer Walk Into a Hospital

Finally arriving at the hospital, the ambulance denizens breathed a collective sigh of relief. Sam and Connor were more than ready to turn their charges over to the nurses greeting them at the emergency department entrance and even Father Randall felt the need to stretch his legs, though he had been in the ambulance less time than anyone else.

Aria and Jack were happy to be emancipated as well. Father Randall's arrival in the rig had spooked Aria and the problem wasn't his demeanor or priestly garb, but rather his bloodied face she found disconcerting. And there was more.

His appearance in the rig brought with it a vision of her sister, a flashback of Steffi's death and its aftermath. Aria had not set foot in a house of worship since Steffi's funeral some six years before, fearing such reflective moments. So, when Father Randall appeared out of nowhere, she was overcome by an all-to-familiar rush of sadness. But Aria was tortured by Steffi's death whether she attended services or not, never having forgiven herself for not recognizing the signs or, far worse, *choosing* not to recognize the signs as her sister hurtled, one final time, down a well-worn path of self-destruction.

At the moment, however, the truth didn't really matter. Ever since Steffi's death, consciously or subconsciously, Aria had feared a reckoning, one that would never come but was as real to her as the snow falling from the sky. Consciously or subconsciously, she had been doing her best to hide from this reckoning, her refuge the space behind a slab of wood and copper effectively separating her, physically and psychologically, from the rest of humanity.

Still, as she and Jack and Father Randall were ushered through the sliding doors of the emergency room, she felt a desire to pull the priest aside and ask him all the questions she wanted to ask back then, all the questions she should have asked, but didn't.

Had it not been for an irrational fear of some sort of as-yet undefined karmic retribution, Aria would have broken from her place in line at the intake counter, cornered Father Randall, and held him hostage until he explained, to her satisfaction, why God allowed Steffi to do what she did.

Of course, she wouldn't demand answers of the priest. Right then she couldn't bring herself to be so bold. She played the scene out in her mind and, horrified, kept her mouth shut and waited in line, sandwiched between Father O'Neal and Jack. She was thankful for her turn at the counter, and received the clipboard and pen with a smile. She was also thankful for the simple instructions handed down by the nurse hiding behind her own counter.

Forms were simple. She could hide in them.

Jack waited in line behind Aria. They had spoken little since falling from the back seat of Sergeant Thompson's cruiser. In the new environment of the hospital, where he wasn't at all sure what might happen, he felt desperate to speak with her, but doubted standing in line at a hospital intake counter was the right time for a chat. They were being watched, and not just by Sam and Connor, who had led them all inside from the rig, and who now appeared to be in deep conversation with some hospital staff. They were now targets in the bullseye of the deputy who had tased Jack on the riverbank. Deputy Lane stood in a corner of the waiting room, cooling his heels, an eagle eye on Jack and Aria as they stood in line. To Jack it was obvious the deputy was there to monitor him and Aria, but he was clueless about what Lane expected to catch them doing, and this lack of information only reinforced Jack's anxiety. He wondered what he had done to instill such determination in the young lawman but couldn't think of anything off the top of his head except, perhaps, his attempt to run downriver after being ordered not to. Still, Jack didn't feel as if that particular little dust-up was enough to inspire this level of attention. Not really, anyway. Plus, Lane had already taken the opportunity to tase him which, from Jack's point of view, squared things up between them and should have been enough to dampen any ill will the deputy might be harboring.

*Maybe he has a problem with people jumping off bridges?*

Jack wasn't sure exactly what dictates were in play when it came to this particular behavior. Did it require a permit? Was it only illegal if unsanctioned by the local authorities? Either way, Jack figured Deputy Lane knew exactly which local statutes governed this category of bridge etiquette, and that for some reason took it personally whenever anyone violated said laws.

Remarkably, though Jack's mind was still quite active, to the average bystander it looked as if he might topple over at any moment. He kept his mouth shut as stood in line behind Aria, ready to receive his clipboard of medical questions. Aria hovered in front of him, attentive as she received instruction from the impassive nurse. Jack was sure the intake nurse had likely handed out these exact same forms thousands of times, and had her instruction speech down to a science. She did not seem at all phased by the crumply mien of the three people lined up at her desk. Not even a bloody priest appeared to be sufficiently out of the ordinary to throw a wrench into her script, so by the time it was Jack's turn to receive a pen and clipboard, he'd already twice heard the recitation.

"Fill out the form to the best of your ability."

*Okay, that leaves a lot of leeway, I think.*

"And bring it back to me as soon as you can."

Having listened intently to the nurse's instructions, Jack, clipboard in hand, was ready to head to the chairs in the waiting room. Next on his agenda was a conversation with Aria, and not just to firm up their version of events, at least not yet. He wanted to hear her voice, hear her tell him she was okay, and tell her that he was ok, too. He wanted to hold her, share a moment like they had experienced on the riverbank, even though he was exhausted, and knew she must be, too.

Father Randall was the first to sit, sighing as he did so, as if this was not his first late-night visit to the emergency room. And it was not his first, or even his hundredth. To Father Randall the waiting room looked almost as familiar as his own living room. During his years in the clergy, he'd spent more than a few nights in emergency rooms, mostly in his official capacity, tending to members of his flock. Not all his trips, however, were undertaken in his role as spiritual shepherd. Father Randall, besides (generally) being able to handle his alcohol, could also be handy in a bar fight. A Golden Gloves ranked boxer as a young man, Father Randall was only occasionally forced to throw a punch, but welcomed those opportunities to do so in the service of God, always protecting someone with his prowess and his faith—a "fighting Irishman" in the best sense.

Jack and Aria sat opposite Father Randall and dove into the forms, if for no other reason than to see what might be the next step in their evening's journey.

69

Jack was nearly halfway through his forms when his attention was drawn to a familiar group of young men across the room. Looking closer, while trying not to be obvious, he recognized them as three of the drunk and disorderly mob of college students he'd encountered on two separate occasions earlier in the evening. They were sitting in chairs along the wall, looking spent and semi-comatose. The rest of their group may have been there, too, but Jack figured they had probably been shuttered away in some other part of the hospital for closer observation.

Jack was surprised, and oddly excited, to see them. He was sure none of them would recognize him, as he had played no more than a bit part to their antics throughout the evening. For Jack, however, the undisciplined underclassmen loomed large in what was to be the final night of his life, showing up twice to offer an element of (mostly) harmless physical comedy to Jack's nocturnal travels. In fact, Jack found the bar fighters' two earlier intrusions helpful. The first violent interaction, occurring only between the students themselves, resulted in some needed weathering, in the form of spilt wine, to a notebook he considered at the time to be too pristine. The second conflict, entailing the students versus a group of husky transvestites, created the distraction Jack needed to ditch his barfly buddy, Kevin, who had glommed onto him earlier in the evening.

The troubled trio were as scruffy and unkempt as he and Aria and, sadly, the fighting frat boys seemed to have lost their verve. They now sat dejected, staring blankly at the ceiling, the floor, or other objects of no particular importance. Clearly, the alcohol purveyors of Cincinnati no longer had anything to fear from them, tamed and shamed as they were, like children sitting in time-out.

Of course, by then all the bars in the city were closed, which may have explained why the rioters were no longer active. Jack suspected the police may have snagged them after the fight with the drag queens, who were physically imposing, more numerous than the students, and likely able to inflict some real damage.

He fought the urge to question them about their evening and how they ended up in this particular waiting room, figuring the opportunity would likely be presented again and, if it didn't, that was okay, too. To Jack, it appeared they were there for the duration. Unfortunately, the same seemed true for him and Aria.

He took time to record the moment.

*2:36 AM*

*Me again, Posterity.*

*I'm writing in this little notebook, and the words are eating up the pages pretty quickly.*

*I may have to write smaller to fit everything in.*

*Anyway, you should know my night has come full circle.*

*The drunk college students are here in the emergency room with me and Aria (and Father Randall.)*

*I want to talk to them but think it would be a waste of time.*

*But why am I so happy to see them?*

*I'll work on an answer to that last question.*

*Meantime I'm happy also Aria's here with me, and that we're both alive.*

*You should also know I'm going to try to do a better job holding on to this notebook compared to the last one.*

*I don't think that was really my fault, though.*

*I mean, I jumped in the freakin' river after Aria.*

*I didn't have time to think. It was a reflex.*

*But the old notebook is gone. This is the new one, for now.*

*I'll look for a bigger one when I get a chance.*

*Now back to medical forms . . .*

Aria did her best to fill out the stupid medical questionnaire but was having a problem focusing. The words on the forms faded and blurred and she had to squint to read them. Jack was distracting as well. As far as she could tell, he seemed to have abandoned any effort to fill out *his* forms and was now just staring at three crumpled guys across the room. Given their disheveled appearance, Aria thought it possible they had been in the river, too. She had no idea who they were, however, as Jack had yet to clue her in as to why he was so interested in them.

But it made Aria happy to see Jack writing in the little notebook she'd coaxed from their new ambulance friends. She had yet to do anything with hers but was pleased she had it, just in case.

The forms were a different story. In every movie or show she had ever seen, people coming into an emergency room from an ambulance were never asked to fill out forms once they arrived. She could only assume she and Jack and Father Randall were not sufficiently damaged to avoid the mindless paperwork.

Part of her frustration was that she did not have her purse, which she believed was still sitting on a shelf behind the bar at Liberty's. She left it there when she left to look for Jack, viewing it as an unnecessary item for hunting, opting instead to take just her phone, a credit card, and her driver's license.

Until that moment, Aria had forgotten those three items were gone. They were in the pockets of the coat she had traded earlier in the evening to her friend Tracy who, Aria was sure, was now safely asleep. Aria was also sure that, had she the means to contact her, Tracy would have abandoned her warm bed without hesitation in order to assist her friend in any way possible.

But Aria didn't know Tracy's number. Aria didn't know anyone's number.

Except her own.

But knowing her own number wouldn't help her now, in the middle of the night, because even if she did try calling it, she was sure Tracy wouldn't hear it. Her cell phone had likely gone unnoticed in the pocket of the wet, wool coat Tracy had worn home.

On the other hand, it was possible Tracy found the phone. Maybe even probable. Tracy was definitely the kind of person who would find a phone in the pocket of a coat that didn't belong to her. Aria pictured her with the coat. It was too wet to hang in the hallway closet. She would put it up somewhere it could dry, but first she would check the pockets, and then—voila!

The phone would likely be damp, maybe ruined, from the water absorbed from the soaked-through jacket. But Tracy—good old, responsible Tracy—would try to fix it. She would put the wet phone in a glass of dry rice, or undertake some other, equally effective, remedy to try and dry it out, at least if it showed any signs of life. But if the phone appeared completely dead she might not have bothered.

Aria crossed her fingers, hoping her phone had some life left in it, that Tracy did find it in the coat of her pocket, and that if she called it her friend would answer.

*That's a big ask, but you never know.*

*Now back to these forms.*

But the desire to fill out medical forms eluded her, so she instead grabbed the little notebook Jack had given her in the rig, stared at the blank first page for a minute, and started writing.

*2:50 AM*

*I wonder if that cop over there would let me use his phone to call my phone. He's just standing there, staring at me and Jack. He doesn't look evil or anything like that, even though I don't think he likes us very much. I'll ask him later, after I'm done with the clipboard forms.*

*Well, damn. Here's a stumper: "Please describe the nature of your injuries." Really? Honestly, I can't even begin to describe the nature of my injuries. Do they mean physical? Psychological? Probably physical. There's only two lines available.*

*Still not sure how to answer, though. Head injury? Three head injuries? I've fallen and I can't get up?*

Aria put the notebook in her pocket, pondered the question a moment longer, and filled in the two lines available on the form.

*I keep hitting my head on stuff. I hit my head on the street, a cast iron pig, and whatever was floating around in the river. Otherwise, I seem to be in decent shape, especially if you don't count about a dozen bruises and cuts.*

Setting aside his new notebook, Jack riffled through the stack of forms held in place on the clipboard, marveled by the stout springs attached to the clamp, impressed with the simple mechanism as only an engineer could be. He was dismayed, however, by the form in front of him, which involved a lot of personal information. Jack didn't have a problem with the easy questions. He knew his address, date of birth and phone number. To Jack, the fact he knew all these basic things about himself somehow proved he hadn't been concussed, despite having been run over by a scooter and taking a short but violent dip in the river.

Despite the temporary distraction of the college students, Jack was impressed by how quickly he was getting through the forms, the volume of which he initially found intimidating. Most of them were a nuisance of one type or another, while others seemed to exist only to announce the existence of another form. A couple were created to declare to the patient what rights they had *as* a patient, and another had to be signed to acknowledge receipt of the one about patients' rights. While exasperating, nothing on any of the forms stumped Jack until he got to the following question: "Describe the nature of your injuries."

*Which injuries?*

Jack thought the question too vague. It provided no time frame for said injuries, nor even the suggestion that his response to the inquiry should have something to do with this particular late night/early morning visit to the emergency room.

Jack decided the implied time frame to be unlimited, let the question stand on its own merits and answered simply:

*I was in a car accident.*

There were only two lines available for the description, so he appreciated the brevity of his response, and hoped the medical staff would as well.

The question in the next box reinforced Jack's conclusion about the last:

"When did you sustain your injuries?"

To that Jack wrote:

*One year ago.*

The deadeye stare from Deputy Lane unnerved Aria, and she allowed it to distract her from her medical forms.

*Crap.*

Besides the distraction of the deputy standing like a statue in a corner, she made the mistake of actually attempting to read most of the disclosures contained in the stack, which she eventually realized was not at all necessary. Still, she continued to skim through them, fearing she might accidentally sign off on a set of circumstances where the hospital staff would be allowed to harvest, without her permission, a kidney or some other mostly-necessary bit of her anatomy.

*Which organs can I live without?*

Aria looked at Jack, now buried in his paperwork, and decided not to indulge the question. Once satisfied her body would not be cannibalized should she appear to be the least bit dead, she did her best to ignore Deputy Lane and complete the stack. She was happy with her description of the nature of her injuries and was about halfway through the next page when this question appeared:

"Do you feel safe at home?"

*What kind of hospital is this?*

Aria circled yes, deigning not to comment further. She lived alone, after all. The only person she had to fear was herself.

She found the next question even more bizarre:

"Are you in need of psychological counseling?"

*What the hell?*

She looked again at Jack, who was staring at the ceiling, in a clear attempt to formulate an answer to one of the questions, maybe even to the same question.

Aria's knee-jerk reaction was to circle "No" and to wonder if she should write "Hell" in front of the "No." To her surprise, however, the question gave her pause, and she thought about it before answering.

*Do I need psychological counseling?"*

Aria's brain, without conscious prompting, kindly replayed the entire evening for her and, by the time she reached the end of the replay, was forced to reconsider the question, wondering how anyone in their right mind would have undertaken the task she had given herself nearly ten hours earlier.

Aria crossed out "Yes" and "No," and wrote in "Maybe."

# Chapter Seven

## Whither Thou Goest

Jack attempted to check on Aria's progress without her noticing him attempting to check on her progress. He failed. She caught him immediately because she was doing the same.

"Did you finish?"

She smiled up from the clipboard. "I don't even know. Maybe? Every time I think I'm finished I find another form."

Jack smiled.

"You?"

"Yeah, I think I'm done now," he said. "Anyway, let's just turn them in, and if we missed anything they can just ask us about it. Better to ask forgiveness, and all that. Plus, don't you have a little story to tell me?"

Aria groaned. She knew exactly what he was alluding to. She'd been dancing around it since they crawled out of the river.

"You want to know about the last time I was arrested. Right?"

Jack nodded vigorously, a little smile tugging at the corner of his mouth. "Yes, and I think now's the perfect time. We're just sitting here waiting for our names to be called."

Aria looked across the room. She was not anxious to share the story with Jack, or anyone. "But Lane's right over there."

"He can't hear you. Now spill the beans, please."

Aria took a deep breath and organized her thoughts. "I don't think I've ever told you about my sister, Steffi."

"No, you haven't."

Aria swallowed hard. "Okay . . . here goes. Well, Steffi killed her-self. She had things going on with her, psychological things. For years. Mom and Dad tried to get her right, and she would be right, for a while. But then she would backslide, and during a few of those times she tried to kill herself." She paused and looked at Jack, seeing she had his full attention. "Finally, she went through with it."

Jack stared at her. "And . . . you still dream about her?"

"Well, yes. Actually, I think about her all the time." Aria stopped short of telling Jack she blamed herself for the death of her sister.

Jack wanted to ask questions about Steffi. Her death clearly hung over Aria like a dark cloud but he did not believe the hospital waiting room was the place to dive in to such a weighty topic. He tried to keep it simple. Or at least simpler. "And . . . you were arrested?"

Aria launched into the explanation. "Okay. It was a few months after Steffi killed herself. Things were kind of out of control for me after she died, you know? I had taken time off from school but I went back because I, well, my parents, thought the structure would help. But I was a mess. I was partying all the time; I was skipping class."

Aria looked up at Jack to see if he looked horrified, but his ex-pression showed only curiosity and caring.

She continued. "It was after a party. I was walking back to my place with four or five people from the party. Everybody was wasted and along the way we started playing Truth or Dare. It started off small, like 'I dare you to ring that doorbell.' But things, you know, escalated, and before long somebody dared me to run naked, up and down the street. So I took my clothes off and started running, right past a cop car parked on the street. I didn't see it because its lights were off."

She paused again. "Long story short, they arrested me for drunk and disorderly, public nudity . . . and a couple of other things."

"That's it? You ran naked down the street? That doesn't sound so bad." Jack thought for a moment. "You said a couple other things?"

"Well, yeah, there's more. When they stopped me, I got a little agitated." Aria paused and looked up at the ceiling. "You know, looking back, I'm not even sure they were going to arrest me, at least not until I started arguing with them. Doesn't matter now, I guess. Anyway, when I started getting agitated, they tried to handcuff me, and that's when things really got out of control. I fought with them. I don't remember everything, but I do remember throwing a few punches. Before I knew it, I was naked in the back of a cop car. My parents had to come and get me out of jail."

"And that's what you're so embarrassed about?"

"Well, yes, but there's more. Not long after I found that one of my so-called 'friends' filmed the whole thing on their phone and put it on the internet."

Jack was upset for her. "Jeez. I think I want to kill that guy."

"It was a girl." Aria stopped to let that sink in. "And it's still out there, as far as I know. I mean, I don't go looking for it, but once it's out there, it's hard to make it go away. Eventually, after a talk with my parents' lawyers, she took it down. But who knows how many times it was copied. At least she didn't put my name on it." Aria paused again. "I've seen it, by the way. It's hard to tell it's me, but not impossible."

Part of Jack wanted to hug her, wanted to comfort her for all she'd been through since her sister's death. But another part wanted to laugh. That part of Jack was picturing a naked Aria in a fist fight with a couple cops. Still, he managed to keep a straight face. "Wow. That really sucks, Aria. I'm sorry it happened."

"I guess, you know, in the grand scheme and all, it's not that big of a deal. But my parents were really embarrassed, and since it wasn't long after Steffi, they automatically thought I was headed to a dark place."

"Were you?"

Aria thought for a moment. "Yeah, probably. It's possible that getting arrested saved my life."

Aria abruptly stood up, grabbed their clipboards and walked them to the intake desk where the nurse, Rita Dolworth, RN (according to her name tag,) waited patiently for something to do.

"Here you go."

Aria smiled at Nurse Rita, who did not return the smile.

"Have a seat and we'll call you when it's your turn."

Aria needed to shake off the images her conversation with Jack brought to mind, and attempted some lighthearted banter with the dour nurse.

"Are there many people in front of us? Any gunshot wounds or stabbings? I imagine they would get first priority."

"Two gunshot wounds and one stabbing. And, yes, they generally get first priority over drunks and car accidents."

Nurse Rita had yet to smile, apparently finding nothing funny or lighthearted in the question, but this only encouraged Aria to try again.

"What if they were shot or stabbed *while* they were drunk or in an accident, or both?"

Aria's attempt at humor continued to evoke nothing in Nurse Rita beyond the professional interest she'd already demonstrated.

"They would still have priority, Miss. Now please go back to the waiting room and wait for us to call you. As you can see, I have a lot of work to do, and I don't have the time to chat."

Aria turned away but caught herself smiling on the way back to the waiting room.

*Did Nurse Rita just make a joke?*

She found the idea immensely pleasurable and, without really be-ing sure if Nurse Rita had made a joke or not, gave herself a mental pat on the back. If she could get a world-weary nurse to joke around with her at three in the morning, what couldn't she do?

Aria carried her unexpected victory with her, back to the waiting room where Jack waited, smiling.

"Naked down the street, huh?"

Aria groaned. "Yes, Jack, naked. If you're lucky, I'll help you look for it."

"What happened over there? You seem a little too peppy for this place. Did you convince them to give us a ride home? Are they going to *not* charge us for the ambulance?"

"Better than both of those things. I got Nurse Rita to make a joke."

"Well, damn. Nice job. Really. Maybe next time you're up there you could work on the 'no charge for the ambulance' thing?"

"We'll see. I'm clearly on a roll."

"Clearly."

Given the series of events that had led the two of them to the emergency room that early Saturday morning, it would have been fair for Jack to question Aria's assertion that she was "on a roll." But he didn't let that stop him from being happy for her, happy she'd found something to celebrate as they sat in uncomfortable chairs, in an uncomfortable room, in an uncomfortable situation.

"Do you think she likes you enough to move us up in line?"

"Hmm...that might be a stretch. Maybe just me? But, you know, in the meantime we can watch the zombies."

"The what?"

"The zombies. Look around, Jack. Everyone here looks as bad as us, or worse. I mean, look at that guy."

Aria kept her hand low but used her left index finger to point at a gentleman with unkempt hair, wearing a stained overcoat, worn jeans and gym shoes. He was across the room, pacing back and forth in front of a window.

Aria quipped. "That guy definitely has the zombie gene."

Jack laughed out loud, drawing the attention of half the room and of Deputy Lane who, as far as they could tell, hadn't left his self-assigned post in the corner.

Lane went back to writing in his notebook, or at least he gave the appearance of doing so. For all Jack and Aria knew, he was scribbling cartoons. What they didn't know was that, in addition to Lane taking it upon himself to keep an eye on the unusual couple, he was doing so on his own time. In fact, Lane had tried to rope Sergeant Thompson into staking them out with him, but his compatriot wanted nothing of it, preferring instead to get home to his wife and dog.

Deputy Lane, on the other hand, lived alone. No girlfriend, dog or cat would notice his presence or absence. For Tommie Lane, going home almost felt like a sort of goldbricking. He could accomplish far more, or at least no less, by keeping an eye on the two nut jobs he first encountered three hours earlier. Should any additional tasing be necessary, he would be there to handle it

"Balfour?"

A new nurse called out the name. She was standing close to Nurse Rita, who was pointing toward the waiting room, attempting to guide her coworker's attention to Aria and Jack. When there no reaction, the new nurse called out again.

"Balfour?"

This time Aria and Jack both heard it, and they stood up together, as if both their names had been called.

"Balfour?"

Aria and Jack walked shoulder-to-shoulder to the nurse's station.

"I'm Aria."

"She's Aria Balfour."

"He's Jack. Jack Current."

The new nurse, who was not wearing a name tag, was unimpressed by the washed-out couple's ability to name each other.

"I only need Aria Balfour. Jack Jack Current, you can go back to the waiting room."

Jack and Aria were confused and looked at each other in alarm. Though neither was quite conscious of it, in the last few hours they'd grown reliant on each other, especially in their new roles as mutual caretakers.

Without having to think about it, the unique experience they shared at the bridge and everything since had bonded them. They had become foxhole friends: Together they'd faced an existential challenge and its ongoing aftermath. The were not ready to be separated.

Jack managed to speak first.

"But we're together."

Aria chimed in.

"Yes, we are. We're together. Me and him. Can't we go back together?"

The nurse sighed and looked at Nurse Rita, who shrugged her shoulders.

"Alright, you both can walk back with me, but I'm putting you in separate exam rooms."

The new nurse turned on her heel. Jack and Aria stood and, after giving a little wave to Father Randall, allowed themselves to be led into the bowels of the emergency department. Looking over her shoulder to make sure they were following, the nurse noted they were holding hands.

*Ugh. Friday nights are always so weird. What I wouldn't give for a nice, calm Monday right now.*

Their shared panic attack now dissipated, Jack and Aria continued to hold hands until the new nurse assigned them adjoining exam rooms, issuing instructions before pulling their curtains shut and departing.

"Get some rest, you two. We're busy, so expect to be here a while. And, don't worry about getting the sheets dirty."

In adjoining rooms, a curtain between them, Jack and Aria were now separated for the first time since Aria found Jack on the bridge, hours ago. But not all hope was lost. There was a gap between the curtain and the wall through which they could spy one another.

"Is yours comfortable?" Aria patted the mattress.

The back supports of their beds were slightly elevated, allowing them to recline.

"Mine's awesome." Jack clasped his hands behind his head.

"Mine, too. Best mattress I've ever been on. But why are hospitals always so cold?" *And uninviting?* Aria pulled the thin sheet and cotton blanket up to her chin and closed her eyes against the glare of the fluorescent tubes raining down from the stained drop ceiling.

Jack smiled at the ceiling and wondered if, at that point in their adventure, any mattress would have felt like the best mattress in the world.

"Seems like we've been awake forever."

Aria heard the words from Jack's side of the curtain. They floated to her as if through a thin layer of water. Throughout her strange evening, Aria had found herself flat on her back or stomach more times than she cared to admit, but all those instances had been uncomfortable. The hospital bed, on the other hand, invited her to close her eyes. Her mind began to drift almost as soon as she laid down.

In the phantasm, Aria was at dinner with her parents and her sister, Steffi. The four were talking about their day, their plans for the next one, and enjoying every minute of it. She couldn't remember ever seeing her sister so happy.

But during the lighthearted conversation, Steffi's demeanor morphed from joy to hostility, felicity to bitterness. The lights in the dining room flashed and dimmed, reflecting Steffi's confusion and enmity. From out of the ether appeared a straight razor, which Steffi brandished, threatening to use it on herself. She was angry, she said, angry at everyone at the table. They had hurt her, she said, and now she was going to hurt herself.

Aria woke to Jack gently shaking her shoulder.

"I think you were having a pretty rough dream. Do you want to talk about it?"

Aria shook her head. She didn't want to talk about it.

"How long was I out?"

"I'm not sure. Not long, I think. Maybe a few minutes. I noticed when you started thrashing around a little." Jack took her hand. "You said your sister's name."

"It's ok, Jack. I'm ok. Thank you."

Aria squeezed Jack's hand, happy she'd added him to the very small circle that knew about Steffi.

*It's not like I go around advertising it.*

In fact, Aria had never told anyone about Steffi, or at least not anyone who didn't have a professional interest, like the shrink she saw after her sister's death, or anyone who didn't already know what happened. And that second category was not overlarge, containing mostly family members and the sisters' school friends. The Balfours, including Aria, had little solace in friends, none in strangers, and saw no point in advertising the circumstances of Steffi's passing. They were not ashamed of it, but they had grown tired of telling the story. It was too difficult.

So it wasn't just him she'd kept in the dark. No one at the bar knew anything about Steffi and that was how Aria preferred it.

Before they could further discuss Aria's nightmare, the curtain to her "bedroom" opened about six inches, and a voice filtered in from the other side. A male voice.

"Is it okay to come in?"

Aria looked at Jack.

"Looks like we're not going back to sleep."

"Hello?" said the voice.

"Yeah, okay to come in."

A man in scrubs entered, along with the nurse who had walked them back from Nurse Rita's intake desk. He, like nearly everyone else, had a clipboard, which he set down on the rolling, adjustable table next to Aria's bed.

"Hi there. I'm Dr. Brown and I'll be taking care of you tonight."

Dr. Brown leaned over the table and addressed a different clipboard.

"Aria? Am I pronouncing that correctly? Aria?"

He was saying it like "Air-y-a."

"Um, well, actually it's Ar-y-a."

"Oops! Sorry about that, Ar-y-a. Better?"

"Yup."

"Great."

Dr. Brown turned his attention to Jack.

"Hi there. You must be..." The doctor flipped through some pages on the clipboard. "Jack. Is that right?"

Something in Jack's brain told him to try and be funny.

"Well, it's pronounced Jock, like Jacque Cousteau."

"Really?"

Jack nodded the affirmative.

Dr. Brown suspected Jack's assertion, but was too busy to question it.

"Okay, then. Well, Jacque, I have to examine your friend here. Do you mind going over to your bed?"

Jack reluctantly did as he was told, using the shortcut between the curtain and the wall to get back to his room. When he was through, the nurse's hand grabbed the edge of the curtain and pulled it shut.

Through the thin layer of cotton separating the two exam rooms, Jack could easily eavesdrop on Dr. Brown's conversation with Aria. It didn't make him happy, and he didn't understand why it didn't make him happy. Was it because another man, a man likely more successful than he, was now getting alone time with his new love interest? Instead of stewing about it, he pulled out his notebook. There were few pages left. He was going to have to find another notebook, sooner than later.

*3:20 AM*

*I mean, holy shit, is she laughing over there?*

*I don't know, Posterity. This whole thing is pissing me off and I'm not sure why.*

*You know what I mean?*

*I swear to God I just heard her giggle. What the fuck is so funny?*

*Is he flirting with her? I can't hear exactly what he's saying.*

*He's probably used to keeping his voice down.*
*I mean, it's just a curtain separating the exam rooms.*
*By the way, not to jump around too much, but there isn't*
*much paper left in this notebook.*
*I'm going to have to go scavenge for another one if I'm go-*
*ing to keep this up.*
*Cops must write really small. Or maybe they use shorthand.*
*I suppose I could ask Deputy Lane? Not sure he enjoys my*
*company.*
*But now I'm wondering what he's up to. Lemme check.*

Jack got up from the chair next to the hospital bed. When Dr.
Brown forced him out of Aria's room, he opted to stay off the bed,
figuring he stood a better chance of staying awake if he was vertical.
He walked to the end of the bed and peaked out the side of the curtain, scanning the room for a body attached to a sheriff's hat. Sure
enough, Officer Lane had abandoned his post in the waiting room,
and was now standing guard just down the hallway. Jack returned to
the chair.

*3:23 AM*
*Well, damn, looks like Deputy Lane is following us around.*
*Not sure what he thinks is going to happen? Do I have a rea-*
*son to run?*
*Is there something I should be running from? Maybe I*
*should go ask him.*
*He's gotta be bored. I mean, he's just been standing around*
*for an hour now. Has it been an hour? Yup.*
*We've been here at least an hour. Maybe longer.*
*I wonder if I should get him a cup of coffee or something.*

*Try to make friends.*

*Maybe I should get myself a cup of coffee.*

*One for me and one for Aria. I wonder if we're allowed to have coffee.*

*Jeez, what are they doing over there?*

Jack leaned toward the curtain. Things were quiet at the moment. Then he heard Aria. "Ouch!"

"Everything okay over there?

"Everything's fine, Jacque."

Dr. Brown's voice was calm and not condescending at all.

"Just replacing the butterfly bandages. We'll want to double check and make sure this cut on your girlfriend's head is clean."

Though he gave it his best effort, Jack couldn't find a rational reason to be mad at Dr. Brown. The good doctor was clearly taking care of Aria, plus he publicly acknowledged their relationship, at least offhandedly, as boyfriend/girlfriend, something Jack and Aria had thus far failed to do.

For that detail, Jack considered thanking him, but thought better of it. He didn't want to disturb Dr. Brown while he repatched the cut on Aria's forehead, the one she received while hunting for him.

*3:26 AM*

*Ok, Posterity, don't let me forget to ask Aria about the cut.*

*I feel bad about it, whether she got it looking for me or not.*

*You know, though, the idea she was worried enough about me to track me down makes me feel good. Hmm. Quite a dilemma, feeling good and bad about the same thing, something I couldn't control one way or the other.*

*I'm just about out of blank pages.*

Jack heard Dr. Brown speaking again and moved as close to the curtain as he could without being noticed.

"It's going to leave a little scar, but it's very clean now, so nothing more to worry about. Now, what else did you bang up?"

"Honestly, Dr. Brown. I don't know. I haven't had a chance to look."

"Okay, I'm going to step out for a minute. You and your boyfriend could use some dry clothes.

*Boyfriend! Yessss!*

"I'll ask the nurse to bring you both some scrubs and once you've changed, we'll have another look and see if there's any other place we need to patch up. I'm also ordering CT scans and X-Rays for both of you. We need to figure out if you sustained any internal body or brain injuries."

"Thanks, Doc."

Jack listened as the swish of the curtain marked Dr. Brown's exit from the exam room, finding the idea of putting on some clean, dry clothing attractive. Until that moment, he figured they would be in their river clothes for the duration of the visit.

*3:28 AM*
*Okay, waiting for scrubs. Maybe they'll help me fit in while I look for a notebook.*
*Fingers crossed.*

# Chapter Eight

## The Great Escape

Jack waited impatiently. He peeked around the side of the curtain and saw the nurse who had entered with Dr. Brown. She was reading Aria's blood pressure and taking her temperature and Aria had an electronic thermometer sticking out of her mouth. When the nurse finished taking the measurements, she spoke to Aria in a hush.

"Listen, sweetie. That sheriff out there says he wants a blood alcohol level on you and your boyfriend over there. Did you know that?"

Aria lowered her voice as well, matching the nurse's conspiratorial tone. "I remember him saying something about it earlier, but I don't know exactly when."

"Well, according to him, we're supposed to get them on both of you and that priest out there in the waiting room."

The nurse stopped talking for a moment, pulled the curtain back an inch, and peered into the space outside Aria's exam room. Deputy Lane was standing near the Nurses Station. The nurse continued in hushed tones.

"Here's the thing. Seeing as how busy we are tonight, that sort of thing can easily get lost in the shuffle, and you two already look like you've had a rough night. Do you think you're okay to have that done now? Or would you rather wait?"

She gave Aria a wink. Aria understood what was being asked of her.

"Thank you for asking. I think I'm okay? But I also think the longer we wait, the better."

"I think so, too. Meantime, the doc told me to go ahead and get you both some scrubs. He thought they'd be more comfortable than hospital gowns. We'll put these dirty clothes in some bags you can take home later. Sound good?"

"That sounds great. I can't thank you enough."

"Sure, you can. Get ready. You've got more tests coming up."

The nurse stood and directed her attention to the curtain separating Aria's exam room from Jack's, behind which he was hiding.

"And you, Jack or Jacques or whatever your name is, I know you're standing there. I'll be back in a minute with some dry clothes and we'll get started on your examination."

Jack's disembodied voice wormed its way through the curtain.

"Um...okay. Thank you, nurse."

He listened for the swish of the curtain to mark her exit and stepped to Aria's bed.

"How are you doing?"

"Surprisingly good, I think. More awake than I should be. How about you?"

"The same. Listen, I need to go find another notebook." Jack held his little notebook aloft. "This one's full, so I'm going to go find another one. I'm sure there's got to be a gift shop or something in the hospital. Or maybe I can find one in a storage closet. We'll see." Jack shrugged, then look concerned. "Will you be okay while I'm gone?"

After everything, Aria was not surprised that her new "boyfriend" wanted to wander around a hospital at 3:30 in the morning. By now, his desire to hunt for a new notebook made perfect sense to her.

"I'm fine, Jack. But how are you going to get past that cop out there? He's keeping an eye on us. You heard the nurse, right? He

93

wants to know if we were under the influence when we went off the bridge."

Jack thought about that moment on the bridge, the moment he jumped in after Aria, and tried to remember how drunk he felt right before he went over the railing, but his memory failed him.

"Do you have any idea why they'd care?"

"No, I don't, but it doesn't matter. What matters is he's there and will probably try to stop you from leaving."

"Hmm...good point. Okay, I'm going to have to find a way to distract him. Any ideas?"

Aria thought for a moment.

"How about this? After we change into scrubs, I'll say I have to go to the bathroom. Once I see that he notices me, I'll take a fall. That should completely get his attention. Then, you make a break for it. With any luck, he won't see you leave the exam room."

Jack smiled. "Are you sure you haven't fallen enough for one night?"

Aria smiled back. "Maybe. But what's one more?"

The curtains whipped open to reveal the nurse, effectively interrupting their scheming. In her arms were two sets of scrubs, non-slip socks, and clear plastic clothing bags.

"Well, Jacques, what a surprise to find you here in *this* exam room."

She handed Jack a set of scrubs and a bag.

"Take these, go back to *your* exam room, change, and wait for the doctor. He will be getting to you shortly."

Jack took what was offered, slipped back into his exam room and did as he was told. Mostly. With the fibers still damp, he stripped out of the odorous clothing he'd worn all night, and slipped into the scrubs. The pants were a little short but, after three-plus hours stuck in

94

wet clingy clothing, the scrubs felt comforting and dry. Had he not been overcome by an overwhelming desire to locate a blank notebook, he would have been more than happy to follow the nurse's instructions. As things were, however, he sat on the edge of his bed, waiting for her to leave Aria's exam room, anxious to implement the escape plan.

Little more than a minute later, Jack, assuming Aria had had sufficient time to change, slipped back into her exam room, only to catch her half-naked. Embarrassed, he immediately turned his back to her. She did the same, but their respective turns were not fast *enough*, and Jack had to pretend he hadn't seen what he'd seen.

Jack spoke at the cloth curtain, hanging six inches from his face.

"Oh my God. I'm so sorry, Aria. When the nurse left, I thought you had already changed, and so I just stepped in here and ..."

Aria was unphased. "Don't worry about it, Jack."

Jack, on the other hand, now felt self-conscious about gazing upon the image, now indelible, of a topless Aria.

Aria continued to speak to Jack's back, smiling. "C'mon Jack, this is hardly the weirdest thing that's happened between us tonight. And you can turn back around now."

Like Jack, Aria was by now wearing a clean pair of scrubs. Unlike Jack, however, hers seemed to actually fit, or at least fit as well as a generic pair of scrubs could fit anyone. She gave Jack a once over, giggling at the three inches of naked ankle exposed between the non-slip sock and the hem of the worn scrub pants.

"It's the pants, right?"

"Well, yeah, they're definitely high-waters. But on the positive side, at least I get to see your ankles. I mean, you got to see my boobs. This is the least you could do."

Jack tried to laugh quietly so as not to garner unwanted attention from the nurse or from Deputy Lane. But once it started it was difficult to stop, and not just because his legs were too long for his pants or that he caught Aria topless. The cropped pants and unintended flash of nudity only added to the absurdity of the entire evening. Given the exhaustion, hunger, and adrenal let-down they were currently experiencing, laughter seemed the only logical response.

To Jack's surprise and joy, Aria gave him a hug. A nice, tight hug. It was unexpected and spontaneous and, he assumed, likely prompted by his preposterously bare ankles.

*This feels wonderful.*

It occurred to Jack that despite the closeness they'd experienced on the riverbank, this was the first time they had ever hugged one another in a standing position. Unfortunately, Jack was forced to release Aria's hold on him.

"I'd really, really love to keep doing this, but I think it's now or never for the notebook thing."

"Oh, of course. Absolutely."

Aria reached up, put her hand behind Jack's neck, and pulled his face down to hers. When her lips met his, both were surprised. This kiss was as good as the last one. Maybe better.

"Kiss for luck."

"Thank you for that." Jack smiled.

Aria took a half step back. "Okay, let's get this show on the road. You go back behind the curtain and get ready. When you hear me fall, and once you're sure Lane is distracted, get moving."

"How will I know when you fall?"

"Oh, don't worry, I'll make a lot of noise." Aria smiled playfully. "Listen. Work as fast as you can, okay? You'll want to be here when it's your turn with the doctor. If you're not back, we may never get out of here."

Jack gave Aria a little, stupid wave, slid back into the other exam room, and waited for the signal.

*3:38 AM*

*Just a quickie. No time to write about the frontal nudity.*

*I only have a page left and Aria and I are about to play a trick, or is it a scam?*

*I don't know. It doesn't matter. I just wanted to say, Posterity, that this is getting good.*

*I think this may be the best night of my life. I hope I don't get arrested.*

*Okay, now I'm really out of paper.*

Jack shoved the notebook and pen into the pocket of the scrubs. Everything felt loose—partly because he was sans underwear, having put it in the bag with the rest of his wet clothes, but also because the scrubs and its pockets were baggy. He worried the notebook could fly out of his pocket at any moment. The problem was easily solved.

"Here, take this for me, please. I don't want to lose it"

Jack whispered through the curtain cloth and held the book out to Aria through the open end by the wall. He couldn't see her, but he felt her take it from his hand.

"Thanks."

"You're welcome."

Aria had the notebook in her hand, but wasn't quite sure what to do with it, so she stuck it under the pillow of the hospital bed, telling herself she would remember to grab it when her time in the exam room came to an end. In the meantime, she had a job to do, and pulled at the curtains where they met at the edge of the runners.

"Nurse? I really have to go to the bathroom."

The nurse who had been handling Aria and Jack pointed toward one of the hallways leading out of the exam area.

"Alright, dear, it's right down that hall on the left."

Aria scoped out the terrain and picked her target. Not ten feet away, in the middle of what would be her path to the bathroom, was another rolling, adjustable table, just like the one in her exam room. But this one was full of medical instruments.

"Thank you!"

Aria was ready. She slipped out from between the curtains and, walking normally, headed toward the bathrooms. It took her only three or four steps to reach the table full of medical instruments. Once there, she dove into her scene, loudly faking a cramp and doubling over as if she were being stabbed in the liver.

Aria had put some thought into the drama she was creating. Initially, she figured the best way to go about it would be to fake a sudden-onset headache, or perhaps behave as if she were having a stroke, but she decided both plans were flawed. The first, and potentially biggest, problem was that they were just about to send her for a CT scan, and any play-acting involving head trauma would only serve to push that process along. It was this thought that convinced her to abandon the headache gambit. Aria was ninety percent sure she didn't have a head injury, and the lack of one on a CT scan would beg a lot of questions. The second problem was that she wasn't exactly sure how to fake a stroke, and thought it best not to have a pretend one in front of a crack team of emergency medical personnel that would likely know the difference between a real stroke and a fake one.

Considering all of the above, Aria convinced herself that tummy trouble was the best option. After all, in her experience, anyone could have a stomach issue. They were almost always benign, difficult to diagnose, and therefore unassailable from a medical perspective. So, Aria let out a loud groan, doubled over, and collapsed to the floor in fetal position. In the process she deftly managed to take the table and its contents down as well. The clink and clang of the metal instruments bouncing off the terrazzo, accompanied by the sharp smash of the toppled table, was enough to bring all attention in the room to Aria. Completely committed to the role, she lay balled up on the floor, amongst the scattered instruments, gently moaning.

Jack, hiding behind the curtain, took his cue and slipped out, whisking past the nurse's station and out into the waiting room, where Father Randall sat quietly, playing Angry Birds on his cell phone. The priest, having demolished yet another poorly constructed pig edifice, looked up from the game long enough to see Jack looking right and left, clearly unsure as to which direction he should go. With a wave of his hand, he caught Jack's attention and pointed him down the corridor to his left. Jack, fearing Deputy Lane would soon notice his departure, took Father Randall's direction without question and went scooting down the hallway in his no-slip socks and clean scrubs. Overwhelmed by his escape and attendant sense of urgency, Jack did not think to question Father Randall on his directional choice, instead blindly relying on the clergyman to put him on the right path. But when Jack hit the next intersection of hallways, he still had no idea where he was or in which direction he was supposed to go.

All he wanted was a notebook.

Father Randall, of course, had no idea what Jack was up to, and so assumed he was looking for a bathroom. Being no stranger to that hospital, the priest knew exactly where the bathrooms were located and sent Jack toward them.

As luck would have it, however, the priest actually pointed Jack in the right direction. The hallway led him toward the gift shop, the shelves of which held abundant amounts of blank paper.

While Jack went in search of an empty notebook, Aria twitched and wriggled on the terrazzo floor, quite proud of her performance. In addition to her bachelor's degree and time as a bartender, her resume included a few bit parts in high school plays and she prided herself on her acting skills. Aria writhed on the floor like a professional soccer player trying to draw a foul, and within seconds she was surrounded by nearly every white coat in the room.

And the helpers included Deputy Lane, who found the incident compelling enough to momentarily forego his role as guardian wallflower and see if there was anything he could do to help. There wasn't, of course. The room was replete with trained medical personnel. Plus there was the fact that Aria wasn't really sick. She didn't really need anything from anyone at that point, other than for them all to give her their attention, and in that she succeeded in spades.

Despite the squirming, however, she was still able to observe Jack's progress until he disappeared down the hall. Once sure he'd cleared the danger zone, Aria allowed a couple of the white coats to lift her to a standing position, at which point she experienced a truly miraculous recovery.

"Thank you, everyone. Thank you."

Once vertical, Aria gently removed the supportive hands from her armpits.

"I think I'm okay. Really. That was probably just a gas pain or something like that."

The offers of assistance continued.

"No, really. Probably just needed to . . . pass some gas."

Aria patted herself on the back for figuring, correctly, that none of the helpers would want to be around for the onset of the next gas attack, and within moments she was left to her own wiles, even by Deputy Lane. He'd been the last to the arrive and first to withdraw from Aria's little show once it appeared she was not yet caught in death's icy grip.

Aria spoke to the backs of the white coats as they retreated. "I think I'll go ahead and lie down again. That whole thing took a little more out of me than I thought."

This she did, but not before slipping into Jack's room and turning off the lights. Aria figured she might be able to convince the nurse that Jack had finally decided to lay down, in addition to giving his room the sort of "leave me alone" aspect that darkness inherently implies.

No one seemed to notice she never made it to the restroom.

Jack was stumped when he reached the next crossroad. There was no one around to ask, even had he been brazen enough to do so. He had little interest in drawing attention to himself, and moved along quickly with his head down, doing his best to blend into the background. The scrubs helped with the blending, but the lack of shoes did not, and though he felt a strong need to get where he was going, at one point he stood frozen for a good ten seconds, wondering which way to go. Suddenly, Jack wanted to punch himself in the face for being so stupid.

*Read the damn signs, you idiot.*

As thousands, perhaps millions, had done before him, Jack looked to the heavens. Sure enough, there was a sign just down the hallway to the right. It said "GIFT SHOP."

Not quite sold on the integrity of his non-slip socks, Jack set a brisk but careful pace down the corridor, and there, just past a bank of elevators, was the gift shop. Another sign, the one on the door, said 'CLOSED."

Consciously, Jack understood it was nearly four in the morning, and therefore unlikely that any retail outlet within the hospital would be open for business. Subconsciously, however, something told him the store would still be the answer to his prayers. The lights were on, so he peeked through the glass door, catching sight of a man. The man was cleaning the floor.

Jack jiggled the door handle and to his surprise and delight it was unlocked. He walked in without pause.

"Excuse me. Excuse me, sir?"

Jack tried to get the man's attention over the whirring of the vacuum cleaner. Failing to do so, he carefully walked up behind the man and touched his shoulder. Startled, the man appeared to jump about six inches into the air before turning to find Jack standing there, staring at him. He turned off the vacuum cleaner, his hand still shaking ever so slightly.

"My God, man. You nearly scared me to death."

"I'm really sorry, sir. I just really need to shop."

He spent a moment examining the young man before him. The scrubs didn't fool him. He was sure he was not looking at a hospital employee, but he was curious.

"Can I help you, young man?"

The maintenance man was at least thirty years older than Jack and wearing wireless earbuds, which he turned off with his finger.

"Um, well, I was just hoping to purchase a notebook and a pen. Oh, and maybe one of those stuffed bears over there."

Jack pointed over his left shoulder. He'd passed the stuffed bears on his way to scaring the maintenance man and thought it would make a nice gift for Aria.

"Son, look around. Does this store look open to you?"

"Well, no, sir. It doesn't. And I know it's late and it's crazy for me to be in here, but I don't have much of a choice. It's hard for me to explain, well, nearly impossible for me to explain. But I really, really need a notebook, a pen, and a Teddy bear. And I'm Jack, by the way."

"Young man, do you hear yourself? Why in the world do you need a notebook and a Teddy bear at this time of night? And you can call me Harvey."

"Well, Harvey, I need the notebook because mine is full."

Jack reached into his pocket to grab the little notebook, but the pocket was empty. He'd forgotten he'd already given the notebook to Aria for safekeeping.

"Okay, well, I don't have it now, but the problem was that it was really small, right? So it didn't take long to fill it. And the bear is for a girl who deserves it. A girl who deserves a bear more than anyone right now."

Harvey, whose heart had finally slowed to its resting pace, looked Jack over again, trying to decide if he was drunk, on drugs, or insane, and if it was worth risking his job just to get rid of him. The man before him was wearing socks but no shoes, scrubs that were too short for his legs, and needed a good scrubbing. And he smelled . . . bad. Harvey was sure there was mud in Jack's hair.

He had no clue as to what Jack's story might be, but what was clear to Harvey was that Jack probably had no money with which to purchase the items, even if the store had been open. But, Harvey rationalized, Jack *could* have taken the items and escaped without him noticing, but had chosen to ask for them instead.

Harvey took pity on Jack.

"Alright, son. Take what you need. And maybe grab a comb while you're at it."

Then Harvey did something even he didn't expect. He reached into his back pocket, pulled out a few dollar bills, and handed them to Jack.

"And go get yourself a cup of coffee from one of the machines. I think you could use it."

Tears welled in Jack's eyes as he took the money from Harvey.

"Thank you, Harvey. Thank you so much."

"Don't think twice about it. Good luck with, well . . . whatever the hell you're up to."

Harvey watched patiently as Jack grabbed a cheap ball point pen, a college ruled, 70-page notebook, and a Teddy bear from the shelves near the checkout counter.

"Don't forget the comb."

"Right. Got it. Thank you again, Harvey."

Jack exited the gift shop. Harvey closed and locked the door.

# Chapter Nine

## We Pass and Speak One Another

After ducking into Jack's room to extinguish the light, Aria decided to take advantage of her fake trip to the restroom to actually use the restroom, and managed to get there without anyone asking what she was up to. Sitting on the toilet, she took the moment of peace to recount the last time she had peed, calculating it had been hours. Though the opportunity to lie in the hospital bed—any bed—was welcome, she found the solitude of the bathroom pleasing. Barricaded behind a locked door, she let the quiet wash over her. She had no desire to sit alone in her exam room, stressing about what Jack was doing and when he might return.

Of course, there were consequences to spending too much time on a toilet, and within minutes her hindquarters were numb, so she finished her business, stood up, and cinched the scrub pants. While welcoming the return of a normal blood flow to her buttocks, she wondered if Jack had had enough time to complete his mission. But, other than a general sense of the passing of time, she lacked a sure way to gauge the exact number of minutes she'd spent hiding in the toilet. She never wore a watch, even under normal circumstances, and her phone, of course, was trapped in Tracy's house. She killed some time thoroughly washing her face, hands, and arms up to the elbow. She cupped her hand under the faucet and drank deeply, until then not understanding the depth of her thirst.

*Must have been all the alcohol.*

Aria stared in the mirror at her reflected appearance. There was nothing for her to do about her hair, reminiscent of a robin's nest, the repair of which would likely require professional intervention. But at least she was able to get the smudges off her face.

This was the first time, post-plunge. that Aria had the opportunity to look at herself in a mirror. She could see some of the bruises and small cuts she'd suffered during her time in the turbulent, debris-strewn current and the slippery slog to dry land. She peered closely at the right side of her face, somewhat swollen but miraculously un-bruised.

She pulled at the V neck of her scrubs to reveal more bruises on her shoulder.

"Must have been when we rammed into that barge." She spoke to her mirror self.

*Fortunately, unfortunately.*

Aria stopped looking, figuring the more she looked, the more damage she would find, something she didn't care to do. She estimated the time she'd spent on washing and contemplating the state of her hair and body had taken no more than two or three extra minutes.

*Maybe just a minute more ...*

Aria decided to try pacing back and forth in front of the sink to kill a little more time. The pacing wasn't easy. The wheelchair accessible privy was a little larger than the average bathroom, but not by much, so Aria was only able to take three steps before being forced to pivot and take three steps in the opposite direction. She did this over and over until she counted one hundred steps, and decided to leave.

As far as Aria could tell, no one seemed to notice her walk back to the exam room, except maybe Deputy Lane, who had returned to his corner. The mess created by her dramatic interpretation of a pained collapse had already been cleaned up by persons unknown, for which she was thankful and a little embarrassed.

Once safely inside the exam room, she peeked around the curtain and was disappointed to find Jack's room undisturbed. A brief panic gripped her.

*What if they caught him wandering around and he got in trouble? What if they put him in another room, or even another floor? Handcuffed him to the bed . . .?*

*Oh, that's silly. Jack seems resourceful. And if there's a notebook to be had in the hospital, he'll find it. And come back to me.*

With that comforting thought, Aria decided it was okay for her to take a break from the drama. Lying on the bed, she dozed off almost immediately, but hadn't been asleep for more than five minutes before the nurse woke her. Thankfully, she hadn't begun to dream, at least not about Steffi. Whatever was going on her head had to have been pleasantly benign.

"Aria? Wake up, sweetie."

The motherly nurse gave Aria's shoulder a light shake and when she opened her eyes, found the nurse with no name tag standing next to the bed.

"Hey . . . Is everything okay?"

"Everything's fine. We're just going to take you up for a CT."

"What about Jack?"

The words came out of her mouth before she realized the potential consequences of the question. The nurse looked toward the curtain.

"He's fine for now. I think he's asleep over there. We'll do him in a bit. Right now, it's your turn."

*Whew!*

Aria swung her legs over the side of the bed and allowed the nurse to lead her out of the exam room to a wheelchair resting just beyond the curtain.

"Have a seat, sweetie. I know you can walk, but rules are rules."

Aria was not at all put off by the wheelchair and actually welcomed it. She was tired, and found the idea of being wheeled from Point A to Point B quite pleasant. The nurse guided her into the elevator, slid in behind Aria, and pushed a button. Arriving on the floor, the number of which Aria had already forgotten, the nurse delivered her to a waiting room. There was a counter just like the ones in the emergency room, and a door behind it.

The sign above the door said: "Computerized Tomography."

*So that's what CT stands for!*

Aria and the nurse had the place to themselves. It was so quiet Aria was convinced the whole place was closed, but there she was, being told by the nameless nurse to hop out of the wheelchair and sit in one of the boring, stationary seats.

The nurse sensed Aria's anxiety.

"Don't worry, someone will be right with you."

Having dropped her patient into the empty waiting room, the nurse disappeared behind a pair of elevator doors. Aria sat alone. As far as she could tell, she was the only living thing on the floor.

Silence flooded in and Aria kicked herself for being afraid to be alone in the empty room. Why should she care if the scan place was open or not? She told herself she was perfectly fine being left alone. She told herself she would be *happy* to sit in that waiting room until the morning shift arrived and either performed a CT or sent her packing. The sound of her name ringing out into the silence interrupted her affirmations.

"Balfour?"

A young man in scrubs like her own, holding yet another god-damn clipboard, poked his head out of the door behind the empty intake desk.

Aria called to him. "That's me."

While Aria was getting her head scanned, Jack was sneaking down the hallway, carrying his prizes in a bag, the ones he had taken, with Harvey's permission, from behind the counter of the gift shop. He felt confident he could figure out how to get back to the exam room without getting lost. Though not sure how long the mission had taken, he was able to venture a guess due to the proliferation of hallway clocks. Eighteen minutes. He was moving quickly.

Jack was impressed with himself. He'd managed to remember every twist and turn of the way back.

As he approached the ER, however, he encountered a problem. How was he to get back to his exam room without drawing unwanted attention? He stopped just short of the door; the same one he had exited some twenty minutes before. He could see Aria's curtain through the window in the door.

*The safe zone. Think. Think. Think.*

Standing there behind the door, Jack was presented with no blockbuster ideas, at least not at first. It did occur to him there must be more than one way to enter and exit any hospital space. It was basic safety protocol. There had to be another way in.

Jack turned, examined the passage behind him, and settled on a circular strategy. The emergency room was now off his left shoulder. He would keep moving or turning left until he found a way back in, hopefully one unmonitored by Deputy Lane. The strategy paid off almost immediately. In just a minute or two, Jack discovered an alternative entrance. Left and another left, and he was looking through the windows of another set of double doors. Through them he could see Lane, whose eyes appeared half-closed. Jack's path was clear, and the game plan simple. He would move quietly and, if questioned, he would say he'd been in the restroom. Easy-peasy.

Jack waited until he was convinced Deputy Lane had nodded off, gently pushed the door open, and silently made his way to the exam room. Other than the time he and his brother Charlie tried smoking a cigarette in the garage, this was probably the sneakiest thing he had ever done, and he was quite proud of the execution. His reward, he told himself, would be the opportunity to lay down, but first he had something to do. Something important. The Teddy bear.

Jack, obscured from view by the curtains, slipped into Aria's exam room to give her the bear, but she wasn't there. He hadn't heard a peep from her side of the curtain, so assumed she was sleeping. But she just wasn't there, and he had no clue as to where she might have gone.

*It's a damn hospital. They've taken her for some test or something.*

Jack left the stuffed bear on Aria's pillow and returned to the confines of his exam room, laying on the bed and forcing his eyes closed. But he could not rest. The blank pages of the new notebook were there, right next to him, on the bed.

*4:12 AM*
*Okay, Posterity, this is a brand new one. A brand-new notebook.*
*It's good. Lots of blank pages.*
*I don't know where Aria is. I went to get this notebook and now she's gone.*

*I also got her a teddy bear. I hope she's not one of those girls who hates teddy bears.*
*I guess I'll find out when she gets back.*
*Speaking of which, when do we think that will happen, Posterity?*
*Random thought—I'm thinking I've grown dependent on her.*
*Not in a crazy way. Not like a stalker.*
*More like close friends that look out for each other.*
*It's probably unfair to her, but she seems ok with it.*
*She's already done so much for me tonight. Teddy hardly seems enough.*
*I wonder if she feels the same.*

The swish of the curtain interrupted Jack's writing.

"Okay to come in?"

"Sure."

Jack figured he had to agree—that in a hospital emergency room it was obligatory to allow whoever it was into his space. He slipped the new notebook under his leg as the nurse slid the curtain open.

"It's your turn, Jack."

*My turn for what?*

"I'm just going to take your vitals and then we'll send you upstairs, just like your girlfriend."

*Upstairs? Where?*

Jack nodded in acquiescence as the nurse wrapped his right arm in a blood pressure cuff.

"Open up, I need to put this under your tongue."

Jack dropped his jaw as instructed and the nurse placed an electronic thermometer under his tongue.

"Hold that there for a minute."

She was practiced and professional. Clearly, she'd performed these same tasks countless times. But Jack was focused only on pumping the nurse for information about Aria's whereabouts without making it look like he was pumping her for information about Aria's whereabouts. So, Jack sat, thermometer poking out of his mouth, waiting for the opportunity. The thermometer beeped, announcing the completion of its task, while the blood pressure cuff, as if by design, released the pressure it was applying to Jack's upper arm.

*Here is my chance. Be nonchalant.*

"So, hey, I must have been asleep or something. When did Aria leave?"

"Like I said, I sent your girlfriend up for a CT scan. Don't worry, you're probably headed up there, too. Depends on what Dr. Brown wants."

"Well, okay, when will we know what Dr. Brown wants?"

"We'll know after he comes in and sees you for himself."

"And when will that happen?"

Jack was trying to be cordial but could hear an unwanted edge creeping into his voice.

"Sorry, sweetie. Look around, it's early on a Saturday morning in a busy emergency room. Unless you're bleeding out, things are just going to happen when they happen."

The nurse wrote down the results of her cursory examination on a form clamped to her clipboard and left the room.

*4:17 AM*
*I'm going to find her.*
*Aria, if you see this, I'm looking for you.*

Jack peeked out. Deputy Lane's head was slumped to the side and his eyes were closed. Jack was amazed he could sleep and remain standing, and took advantage of the opportunity to make his exit.

Aria had never had a CT scan and, once ensconced in the bowels of the machine itself, didn't understand what all the stink was about. It was loud, for sure, but she didn't care. For whatever reason, she found being stuck for a few minutes inside the machine quite enjoyable, her only responsibility to lay there and keep still.

"So, anything weird going on with my brain?"

Aria was speaking at the tube. The technician told her he could see and hear her on screens in the little control room, and that Aria would be able to hear him as well.

"Oh, well, not sure," the technician said. "You'll have to wait until somebody reads your film."

"And that's not you?"

"Nope. I'm just here to operate the machine. Stay still, please."

Aria stopped asking questions, at least for the moment. In her previous experiences with modern medicine, she had come to realize that direct questions were rarely answered directly. She found this frustrating but understood that badgering a reluctant technician on the sturdiness of her brain's architecture would do nothing to alleviate that frustration.

Once the CT scan was complete, she allowed herself to be helped down from the table and escorted to another wheelchair, happy to again get pushed around the hospital and gently deposited back in her exam room. Upon her return, she was given instructions to wait in her room until the next contact with a medical professional, the timing of which was unknown.

Aria couldn't miss the Teddy bear sitting on her pillow. She grabbed the bear and gave it a hug, enjoying the clean softness of it. The little pad of paper, the one the paramedics had given Jack, had been lying beneath it. There was no card to announce who had given her the gifts, but there didn't need to be.

Aria was overwhelmed by the gesture. She wanted to thank him, to hug Jack and feel him close to her, but when she peeked into his room, his bed was empty, except for a new notebook. Aria grabbed it and opened the cover, her eyes laser-focused on Jack's last line.

*"I'm looking for you."*

She cuddled the bear and read the few sentences Jack had written in the new pad, feeling every word, feeling it with him. She set it back down but couldn't take her hands from it. She wanted to respond, but when she looked around the room for something to write with she found nothing.

*Jack must have taken his pen.*

She needed a pen, or a pencil, or a marker, anything she could use to write back to Jack.

*Where are all the damn pens? Are they all attached to clipboards?*

Aria knew just who to ask, and took an innocent walk to the nurse's station.

"Excuse me. Hi. Do you have an extra pen I could borrow for a few minutes?"

The nurse pulled a cheap Bic ballpoint out of a box of at least twenty and handed it over to Aria with a tired smile.

"Here you go. Keep it."

Aria, watching Deputy Lane from the corner of her eye, slipped back into the exam room and grabbed the notebook from the bed. It took her a few minutes to begin. Getting started was not easy. She wasn't exactly sure who she was writing to, or for, or why. She didn't even fully understand what she was doing. She took a moment to let her thoughts work.

Finally, she put pen to paper, and words began to appear on the page. She imagined she was writing to Jack. It seemed the safest place to start.

*4:21 AM*

*Jack, I have never kept a journal, or written anything, really. School papers. Crap that didn't matter, not to me, really. Maybe to someone else. For a grade.*

*I have to tell you something. I am not sorry I read your notebook in the bar. I know you were trying to keep everybody from seeing it. I didn't understand why, exactly, but I wanted to help, so I read it when I got the chance. You were talking to Fireman Jack or whatever and I took it into the bathroom and managed to read some of what you had written.*

*That's why I followed you. I was scared. I was worried you would hurt yourself.*

*So, I followed you. And I found you. I was so happy to find you.*

*I know you're looking for me right now. I'm coming for you, too. I'll find you again.*

*Don't worry.*

Aria stuck her new pen in the spiral binding of the notebook and set the pad on the bed. She was determined, again, to find Jack.

*This is just one building. How hard can it be?*

Aria propped Teddy on the pillow and tucked him in—something she'd always done as a child with her stuffed friends—turned off the exam room light and peeked out from between the curtains. Now

Deputy Lane was sleeping in a chair against the opposite wall, his overzealous sense of duty overcome by boredom and lack of sleep.

Aria walked out the door, having no idea which way she should go. It struck her it was possible Jack was told she'd been sent upstairs for the scan, and that it would be logical for him to start his search there. With that in mind, she made her way to the same elevator she and the nurse used earlier. The CT Scan floor was listed on a panel in the elevator, along with all the other departments the elevator served.

*Hopefully, it was this easy for Jack.*

She pressed 'Up" and waited for the car.

Aria was alone and, unlike the close quiet of the restroom, she found the emptiness of the hallway as eerie as she had the CT waiting room. She reminded herself it was nearly 4:30 in the morning and that, barring an earthquake, nuclear war, or some other mass disaster, most hospitals wouldn't have much going on at that time of the day. Still, something about the silence made her anxious to find Jack and to get back to their exam rooms.

The elevator arrived and she stepped aboard, hitting the floor number as she entered. The sliding doors functioned at a snail's pace, however, so Aria pressed the '2' button a few times, suspecting it wouldn't make the elevator move any faster. At least it gave her something to do until the doors finally closed.

When the doors opened on the second floor, Aria was pleasantly startled to find Jack standing right in front of her, looking as surprised as she, but smiling. Aria returned the smile, overjoyed to see him but not exactly sure what to say.

Notable was the lack of a smile from the security guard standing to Jack's left, one hand gently laying on Jack's shoulder. In other circumstances, Aria might have been surprised.

"Miss, do you know this gentleman?"

"Sure do."

Aria reached out and took Jack's hand.

"Do you need me to keep an eye on him?"

"That won't be necessary, miss. I'm just escorting him back down to the ER."

The guard gave Aria a once-over and pointed at her socks. "Where I suppose you belong as well. Shall we?"

The guard motioned toward the elevator with his free hand and the three of them piled in and descended. She and Jack were still smiling when the security guard walked them into the emergency room, where the staff there greeted them warmly. One person, however, was not pleased.

Deputy Lane had woken from his slumber.

# Chapter Ten

## Miles To Go Before I Sleep

Jack and Aria were back in their respective exam rooms, though not their respective beds. Separated by the thin, hanging cloth, they stood across from each other, observing the conversation between Dr. Brown and Deputy Lane. Neither could hear a word being exchanged, but the body language of the two uniformed professionals clearly indicated the dialogue was less than friendly. Across the room, in what had become Deputy Lane's favorite observation point, the doctor and deputy squared off in hushed but terse tones.

Finally, an agreement seemed to have been struck, and Deputy Lane's expression suggested he was on the losing end. Dr. Brown turned on his heel and walked toward their exam rooms as Jack and Aria scrambled to get back into their respective hospital beds.

Dr. Brown's hand showed up on Jack's curtain first.

"Okay to come in?"

The doctor's voice was not as calm as it had been earlier that morning.

"Uh, sure."

Dr. Brown entered and stared at Jack long enough to make him uncomfortable.

"Is your girlfriend awake?"

Jack nodded.

"Then, can you please ask her to come in here?"

Jack started to move but before his feet hit the floor Aria was standing between him and Dr. Brown. She'd heard the exchange and was hoping he would give them a blow-by-blow recap of his conversation with Deputy Lane.

"Do you want to sit down?" Dr. Brown motioned to the chair next to Jack's bed.

"No, I'm good, Doc. Thanks. What's going on?"

Aria stayed put, as did Jack, his legs still dangling off the side of the bed, like a toddler in an adult sized chair.

"Well, you two—that's for sure. Apparently, security caught both of you sneaking around the hospital."

Jack and Aria made eyes at each other, as if they were two kids caught with their hands in the cookie jar.

"Now, I talked to the security guard, and my understanding is that you haven't done anything more than wander around. Is that correct?"

Jack and Aria each gave the doctor a nod, hanging on to every word, waiting for him to let them know their fate.

"Here's the thing. That deputy out there wants to take you into custody. He thinks you either jumped off the bridge because you were running from someone, or that you did it because you're stupid, which, in my humble opinion, is not a crime, at least not in this country. If it's the former, he wants to know who you were running from and why. If it's the latter, he said he wants to charge you for jumping off the bridge or, in other words, charge you for being stupid."

Dr. Brown paused to make sure his patients were grasping his words.

Jack leaned in to whisper to Aria.

"I could do life for being stupid."

"Don't worry, I'll visit you."

Dr. Brown coughed, interrupting Jack and Aria's private comedy routine. "You know I can hear you, right? I'm standing right here."

Jack continued. "So, Doc, not to reinforce Deputy Lane's theory about our stupidity, or mine, to be specific, but is it actually *illegal* to jump off a bridge?"

Dr. Brown hesitated.

"I know you're a doctor and not a lawyer," Aria said, "but what do you think?"

"As far as I know, yes. At least in Cincinnati."

Dr. Brown paused again and looked at Aria.

"Alright then. I have a different theory. Here it is. My theory is you both jumped on purpose, but not because you were running from anyone. My theory is you were both trying to hurt yourselves, or worse, that you have some sort of suicide pact. For that reason, I'm not going to let you be arrested, but you have to promise not to cause me any more headaches. No more sneaking around the hospital in scrubs. The staff find it confusing, like you work here, and if I have to, I'll take the scrubs and make you both wear hospital gowns."

Dr. Brown came close to snickering at the idea of putting the two of them in hospital gowns, but Jack and Aria were taking their current and potential circumstances, as Dr. Brown described them, quite seriously. Not the least harrowing of which was the prospect of having to wear a traditional hospital gown, an idea neither found appealing in any way. They, quite naturally, preferred their butts unexposed.

Jack spoke again. "Thanks for being up front, Doc. What do you need us to do?"

"Well, as I said, first thing is no more meandering around the hospital. It's annoying and I've got better things to do than pick fights with the Sheriff's Office."

"What's the second thing?"

Without thinking, Aria moved closer to Jack.

"The second thing is the CSSRS. You both are going to take it. If you refuse, I'll let the deputy do whatever he thinks needs to be done."

Jack and Aria spoke more or less in unison.

"What's the CSS . . . SRCS . . . CRS?"

"Glad you asked. *CSSRS* stands for the Columbia Suicide Severity Rating Scale."

Jack laughed nervously. "So, you think we were trying to kill ourselves?"

Dr. Brown pondered Jack's question.

"I'm not sure, but what I do believe is that you two were not on that bridge by accident, and that you going into the water was no accident either, whether you were trying to kill yourselves or not. So, you're going to take the test and we'll see what we see."

Jack and Aria realized resistance was futile. Their choices were to take the test or get arrested, and getting arrested sounded the least fun of the two options. Aria squeezed Jack's hand and turned to Dr. Brown.

"Alright, Doc, we'll take the test. And thanks for looking out for us."

Dr. Brown smiled. "Well, you're welcome, but let's see how you feel about everything *after* the test. Getting arrested might have been easier.

"Okay, here's how this is going to go down. Shortly you'll each be interviewed by a nurse. Depending on how that goes, you might have another interview with a different nurse."

Aria was intrigued.

"What kind of nurse? The second one, I mean."

"A psychiatric nurse." Dr. Brown paused. "Are you both ready?"

Aria and Jack nodded 'yes' without really believing it.

121

"Okay, then. I've got to go stitch up a priest's forehead. You two just hang loose until the nurses can make time for you."

Dr. Brown left the exam room with a swoosh of the curtain, leaving Jack and Aria to ponder the conversation. Their first thought was to strategize a coordinated response, the way they had in the back seat of the sheriff's cruiser, a moment which, by then, seemed to have happened in the distant past. With Dr. Brown and the nurse gone, however, they had a moment of privacy, and a feeling of closeness they hadn't experienced since their time in that back seat, the foggy glow of the windows shielding them from the world outside. And neither feared being interrupted now, though shielded only by the thin hospital curtain, having been told, for the first time, exactly what would happen next and believing that the thing happening next wouldn't happen right away.

Before the curtain stopped swaying, Jack slipped off the bed and pulled Aria to him. She did not object, and pulled him to her as well. Despite their baggy design, the thin material of the scrubs allowed them to feel the contours of each other's body. Though their first embrace—on the edge of a river, during a snowstorm, in wet winter coats—had an unmistakable thrill, this one was infinitely more enjoyable.

They did not kiss.

Instead, they rested their heads on the shoulder of the other and allowed themselves to again bask in their collective warmth. But they understood their time alone was limited. There was no lock on the curtains.

"Jack." Aria spoke to his shoulder. "Do you want to talk about what we're going to tell the nurses?"

"No."

He pulled her tighter.

"Okay, yes. I guess we should, but I've got no idea what they're going to ask. I've never taken a suicide test before."

"Me neither. I'm thinking we shouldn't cop to any of it, and for sure don't tell the truth about what you were doing on the bridge. They'll take you away if you tell them the truth."

Jack reluctantly released Aria.

"You're right. Let's stick to our story. We were on a date and thought it would be romantic to walk across the suspension bridge in the snow."

"Right, and it was icy, and I slipped and fell over the rail."

"And then I jumped in right after, you know, to try and save you—like any hero would do."

Aria looked up at him.

"That's the truth, though Jack, at least the last part. You did jump in to save me."

Jack mostly believed that was true, but there was a nugget of doubt, and that nugget was wondering if he actually jumped in not to save Aria, but to finish the job he'd started. He did his best to ignore the nugget. He preferred the hero angle.

"Okay. That's what we'll tell them." Jack pulled Aria back into him. "Thank you, Aria."

She didn't question his cryptic "thank you," she didn't have time. The mystery nurse, the one who had been taking care of them since they arrived, walked in before she had a chance.

"Alright, you two. Time for the test. I'm going to get started with one of you and another nurse will be over in a minute to do the other. Which one of you wants to go first?"

Their non-response was simultaneous, internal, and identical. Neither.

But then Aria tentatively held her hand aloft, as if she was responding to a teacher's question but was unsure of her answer.

"I guess I'll go first."

"Okay, you and I will go into your exam room."

The nurse turned to Jack and pointed at the chair next to the bed.

"You stay here. Another nurse will be in shortly."


Aria was proud she volunteered to be tested first, for the second time that morning, but admitted to herself she would have been equally happy had Jack done so.

This test seemed more dangerous than the last one.

"Is this okay?"

Aria reclined on the hospital bed in her exam room.

"Absolutely. Honestly, it won't take long. It's a short test. Shall we get started?"

"Ready when you are."

Aria didn't feel at all ready. Exhaustion stalked her; she was fading as the morning's excitement dissipated. Oblivious, or perhaps indifferent, to her exhaustion, the nurse started pelting her with questions almost immediately.

"Okay, first question: Have you wished you were dead or wished you could go to sleep and not wake up?"

The frankness of the question startled Aria. Even though this was her first ever suicide test, she somehow expected them to be more subtle.

"Um, no. No way."

The nurse circled "no" on the form.

"Question two: Have you actually had any thoughts of killing yourself?"

"Nope."

Aria responded quickly but then thought about what was being asked of her.

"Well, you know, doesn't everybody?"

"What do you mean, Aria?"

She had the nurse's full attention.

"I mean, well, I guess I mean everybody has 'suicidal' thoughts sometimes, don't they? Like, 'Goodbye, cruel world. You suck.'"

To emphasize her point, Aria put the back of her hand to her forehead, leaned her head back, and closed her eyes, feigning despair. She hoped the nurse would find this amusing. She did not.

Then Aria added, "Haven't you?"

The nurse took a moment to respond.

"You know, I can't really say. Maybe. I suppose it's possible but, honestly, I don't remember." She smiled at Aria. "When I think about dying it's really just about my husband."

The nurse paused for a moment of self-reflection, circled "yes."

"Okay, enough chit chat, I think. This isn't about me. Let's move on: Have you been thinking about how you might do this?"

"Kill myself, you mean?"

"Yes."

"Hold on. Did I say I was thinking about killing myself?"

The nurse addressed her notes.

"Well, yes. In a roundabout way, but still a 'yes.'"

Aria was intrigued and confused. It was almost as if the nurse was manipulating the test against her, as if she wanted her to be "positive." Of course, Aria intended to manipulate the test as well, in the other direction. But it appeared, in some way, she couldn't stop herself from at least alluding to the truth.

*Wait. Is that the truth?*

"Well, if I was going to kill myself, it sure wouldn't be from jumping off that stupid bridge, you know what I mean?"

Aria nudged the nurse's shoulder with her elbow.

"You see how well that worked out, right?"

*Shut up! Shut up! SHUT UP!*

Jack had been doing his best to listen through the curtain. His nurse hadn't shown up yet, and he had nothing better to do than to eavesdrop on their conversation. Like Aria, he was shocked at the frankness of the questions. In some ways, he wished he'd gone first. It would have given Aria the opportunity to hear the questions before she was asked, but now he was formulating his own answers.

*Is that bad? Shouldn't I be as up-front as possible? Wait. What the hell am I thinking? Of course I'm not going to be up-front. I'm going to lie.*

He told his brain to shut up and turned his attention back to the words filtering through the curtain into his exam room. The nurse's voice was clear while Aria's was modulating up and down, making some of what she said more difficult to hear. Jack thought he heard her laugh at one point, but it happened at the same time a heart monitor started raging in the exam room on the other side of his. He hoped whoever was attached to the monitor was okay, but he really wanted to hear what was going on with Aria and the nurse. Unable to discern anything through the din, he grabbed his new notebook.

*4:45 AM*

*I hope she's okay over there.*

*I can hear the questions but not her answers. Not all of her answers, anyway.*

*I'm a little torn because I want to listen and I know I shouldn't, so, I'm writing in this instead, while I wait for the nurse to show up.*

*To be honest, Posterity, I'm kind of afraid of taking the test.*

*I don't want to say anything stupid or anything that will get me in trouble.*

*I don't want to tell them the truth.*

*Really, all I want right now is to get the hell out of here with Aria, take her home and get some sleep.*

*I really think we just need some sleep.*

*I know I do.*

*And don't weird things start to happen in your brain when you're sleep deprived?*

*I'm sure I read that somewhere.*

Jack was interrupted by Nurse Rita of the intake desk, who pulled the curtain open and stepped in without asking for permission. She silently reviewed Jack's chart without bothering to ask what he was writing in the notebook.

"Jack Current, right?"

"Nurse Rita, I presume."

"Right. Well, listen, Jack. I'm going to give you this test. I trust Dr. Brown has already explained what it's about?"

"He has."

"Then let's get started."

Nurse Rita was all business. Jack wondered who was out there now, intaking patients, while she was in his exam room, asking him questions about suicide, but wasn't about to ask. He wanted to get the test over with and was determined not to get bogged down in idle chit-chat with a terse nurse who didn't seem to like him very much.

While Jack waited for Nurse Rita to begin, he reconsidered his original strategy, the one he and Aria had agreed upon. Nurse Rita was all business—she might not easily fall for his lies. If that were so, he would have to try something else. His mind raced as she took the seat next to his bed, questionnaire and clipboard at the ready.

"First question: Have you wished you were dead or wished you could go to sleep and not wake up?"

Jack balked, then employed a strategy of redirection.

"Have you?"

"Really, Mr. Current? Are we going to play games?"

Jack rapidly re-reconsidered his strategy and, instead of the old "answer a question with a question" gambit, decided to go back to the original plan. Lie.

"No."

"'No' to playing games or 'no' to wishing you would fall asleep and never wake up?"

"Both."

*Okay, that was easy. I'm really good at lying.*

"Listen, Mr. Current. You can lie, and I'll put down whatever you say. But if you're lying, you should think about why you feel you have to lie."

*Ooh. She's good.*

"Uh, well. I stand by my answer."

Jack wondered, with some alarm, how he ended up with Nurse Rita and not with a nurse more like the one who was questioning Aria. As far as Jack could gather from the conversation in Aria's room, her nurse was far more accepting of her responses, of *her* lies. Jack wondered if Nurse Rita ever worked for the FBI.

"Okay, then. Next question: Have you actually had any thoughts of killing yourself?"

Nurse Rita affixed her gaze at the side of Jack's face. He couldn't see her stare, didn't want to see her stare, but he could *feel* it.

"Yes. No, wait. I mean no. Well, what I mean is, doesn't everybody at some point in their lives? I mean, not to sound like an ass, but haven't you? Haven't we all been there at one point or another?"

"Alright, Mr. Current. I'll humor you for a minute. Go on."

"Okay, I mean, how many people think about it but would never do it? I feel like it's almost everybody, at some point in their lives. I imagine most people can remember a time when they've reached the end of their rope, you know, when they feel they can't go on. But, obviously, most people don't follow through."

"Were you following through, Mr. Current?"

Jack paused, fingering the notebook lying next to him on the hospital bed.

"No. I went in the river for Aria."

Aria stopped talking and stared at the ceiling. She wasn't sure what power the nurse had over her life at the moment, and she feared walking into a trap. No one had asked her questions like these before. Even the therapist, the one she went to see after Steffi's death, never asked her if she might be having the same thoughts as her sister. But even if the therapist had asked the questions, Aria knew she would have denied them. And probably truthfully. After bearing witness to her sister's self-destruction, she trusted she had no desire to repeat it, and refused to think about what that would have done to their parents.

Aria watched as the nurse made notes on the questionnaire.

"So, Aria. I get that you don't like the bridge idea, but do you have any idea how you *would* do it if it came to that?"

Aria wasn't sure she wanted to answer, but worried that not answering was somehow worse than answering, no matter what answer she gave. She was exhausted and her faculties were suffering. She wanted to take a moment and think about an answer to the nurse's question, but she was distracted, and instead of staring at the ceiling, stared instead at the curtain separating her from Jack. His voice was bleeding into her exam room and she wanted to hear what he was saying but couldn't make out his words. She'd catch bits and pieces, but not enough to connect anything together. It took all her willpower to keep herself planted on the bed and not find a way to get closer to the curtain.

"Aria, did you hear the question?"

The nurse's voice startled Aria back into the moment.

"Uh, yes, absolutely."

"Okay, good. Do you want to answer it?"

*Not really. What I really want to do is go over there and listen to Jack.*

"Sure. But I don't really have an answer. I mean, I don't walk around thinking about how to kill myself, if that's what you're asking. All I was trying to say was that, clearly, jumping off the bridge isn't as easy a way to go as people think it is."

"What do you mean 'as easy as people think it is?'"

Aria was frustrated.

*Why doesn't this nurse understand what I mean?*

"Okay, earlier tonight I fell off the bridge. Jack and I fell off the bridge. Sort of. But here we are, still alive. So, the point is, if I was making a list of ways to kill myself, I would cross out 'Jumping Off a Bridge.' It didn't work."

The nurse made notes before looking up at Aria.

"So how would you do it?"

*Aaagh!*

Aria looked at the curtain, waiting for Jack to swoop in and distract the nurse, who just cleared her throat in an effort to prompt an answer to her question.

"Okay, I'm not saying I would, or that I know *how* I would. I just know I would *not* jump off a bridge. So, if you're asking what suicide method I would use, well, I can't answer that. All I've done is eliminate the bridge option. Make sense?"

The nurse finished making a note on the suicide questionnaire.

"Perfect sense, sweetie."

# Chapter Eleven

## Psych 101

"Okay, I think we're done here, Mr. Current."

Nurse Rita had a bit of a scowl on her face, though Jack didn't notice.

"Is that good or bad?"

Nurse Rita stood up.

"It is decidedly neither. However, I'm going to refer you upstairs for further evaluation."

"Upstairs?"

The word made Jack anxious.

"What do you mean 'upstairs?' What happens upstairs?"

"Like I said, Mr. Current, further evaluation is what happens upstairs."

Nurse Rita was either ignoring or failing to recognize Jack's distress.

"Well, I'll be honest, you're not giving me much to go on. I mean, do I *have* to go upstairs? Can't I just leave? Am I under arrest or something?"

Jack's mind was replaying an intense scene from a cop show he'd seen recently. He imagined himself in a windowless room, populated only by a table and a few chairs, being relentlessly questioned by an old-school detective under a dangling, bare light bulb.

"No, Mr. Current. You are not under arrest. But I highly recommend you comply. If you don't, we can compel you to do so. It's better if you do it voluntarily."

"Do what voluntarily? What happens if I don't?"

Somehow, Nurse Rita managed to simultaneously project a demeanor of boredom *and* frustration and made no effort to hide it from Jack.

"You should know that we can put you on a 72-hour 'hold' without your consent. That's why I suggest you voluntarily allow one of our psych nurses to interview you further. If she doesn't see a problem, well then, no problem."

Jack's mind raced. He definitely heard the words emerging from Nurse Rita's mouth, but wasn't sure he actually understood them. Was this something that was within their power? Could they actually keep him there if he didn't answer questions in a way that satisfied them? Had he accidentally been transported to communist China? Jack worked to compose himself before saying anything else. Nurse Rita stood at the edge of the exam room, apparently waiting to see if Jack had any more stupid questions.

"Well, I guess alright then."

Jack said the words without feeling them. He hadn't been this confused since the accident that killed his nephew, Troy. Though, really, the only thing that day and this one had in common was the hospital.

Things were looking all too familiar.

"So, that's a yes. I'll finish my write up and send you upstairs after you've had a CT scan and we do a blood alcohol level."

"Jeez, how long is all this going to take? That sounds like a lot of stuff."

Nurse Rita stiffened.

"It will take as long as it takes." She turned on her heel, exited the exam room, closing the curtain behind her.

Aria, still frustrated the nurse was unable to understand what she was trying to explain about the suicide stuff, could clearly hear Jack's voice, if not exactly all the words he was saying. He was less than six feet away. His tone was wary, and the volume had increased.

While her nurse scribbled something on the suicide test, Aria turned her attention to the curtain, believing if she stared at it hard enough, she would be able to hear exactly what Jack was saying. Though that wasn't the case, it was nevertheless clear that the back-and-forth between Jack and Nurse Rita had become strained. While she listened, Nurse Rita's voice moved a couple feet, and Aria reclined her bed so she could get a look at Jack through the empty space between the edge of the curtain and the wall.

She could see him. He had a confused look on his face and was gesturing with his hands as he talked. Aria couldn't see Nurse Rita, but given the direction in which Jack was looking, she must have been somewhere near the end of his bed. She concentrated harder, attempting to conjure special listening powers, but the sound of her nurse's voice snapped her back.

"Alright, Aria. Let's talk about what happens next."

Her nurse finished her notes and was ready to talk, abruptly ending Aria's spying.

"Sound good?"

"Sure."

Aria readied herself to be as tense as Jack sounded moments earlier. As far as she could tell, however, her nurse seemed a lot nicer than Jack's—the dour Nurse Rita from the intake station.

"Okay, first things first, are you ready for your blood alcohol test?"

Aria gave herself a quick internal examination and decided she was sufficiently sober.

"Yes. I think so."

"That's good. That should get rid of that deputy that's been standing around out there. He's kind of freaking everybody out."

Aria winced.

*Some more than others.*

Deputy Lane's presence had been annoying, in some ways threatening, since Aria first saw him in the waiting room of the emergency department. She felt getting rid of him would go a long way to lowering her stress level, and that if giving a little blood would make that happen faster, she was all for it.

"Is that it?"

"No, sweetie. There's one more thing. I'm going to send you upstairs for further evaluation. I'm a little worried about some of your answers on the CSSRS."

The nurse used the acronym CSSRS as if she expected Aria to remember what real words each letter represented. But she was more concerned with what she was being told by the nurse than by the fact she didn't know the meaning of a bunch of letters. Her heart rate rose a little and she now believed she understood why Jack might have been getting upset over in his exam room. One word, in particular, made her nervous.

"What do you mean, 'upstairs?'"

"That's where the psych nurses are located, and they are more qualified than I am to dig a little deeper into your answers to the CSSRS."

While she believed her nurse well-intentioned, Aria decided she would stab her in the chest with a pen if she said the letters CSSRS one more time.

"What does that mean for me?"

"Well, nothing, really. At least not yet. Their job is to ask you more questions and then determine if you need more time to talk about what's been bothering you, not just tonight, but maybe in general, like with your whole life."

*My whole life? What's been bothering me? Well, THIS is bothering me.*

Aria worked hard to keep her breathing steady and looked around the room for a pen. She wondered if her nurse thought her an idiot. She had to unclench her teeth in order to speak.

"Can you just tell me what's going on, please?"

The nurse set her clipboard down and looked directly at Aria.

"Okay, listen. If those nurses up there determine you're a danger to yourself or others, then they can put you on a 72- hour hold for further evaluation. If you want to avoid that, then don't give them the same, dumb, rambling answers you gave me a few minutes ago. Honestly, I think you're probably okay, and I wrote that on the test, but your answer triggered the next step, and I've got to cover my ass, and the ass of everyone else here in the hospital. Got it?"

In equal measure, Aria was impressed and horrified by the straightforward lecture she received from the nurse. There was no way she was going to allow herself to get stuck in the hospital for another three days, especially if it meant getting peppered with questions about her *whole* life.

"Okay. I understand. Thank you for explaining everything. Let's get on with it."

"Blood test first. Someone will be in here to do that in a few minutes. Got it?"

"Got it."

Deputy Lane had had enough. He'd been at the hospital for hours and was frustrated he didn't possess the power to compel the medical staff to do his bidding and take the damn blood alcohol level of his would-be detainees. He checked his watch and groaned. It was already past five and even though he considered himself dedicated and had no one waiting for him at home, he was sure he could find a better use of his time than standing around an emergency room for hours on end.

From his position against the back wall, he could see the doctor and nurses going in and out of the exam rooms containing his suspects, or at least he could while his eyes were open. He was sure he'd dozed a few times already, and had since fortified himself with coffee from the staff break room.

Deputy Lane watched as the two nurses entered the exam rooms, still carrying their stupid clipboards. He recognized them as the ones he had earlier implored about getting the blood tests done as soon as possible, lest the passing hours give their livers enough time to clean their blood and skew the results of the test in their favor. At the time, the nurses told him they would get right on it, as soon as they were done with administering CSSRS. Lane didn't know what CSSRS stood for and when he asked was told only that it was a suicide test. Regardless, he was starting to think the nurses had been somewhat less than honest about when the tests might be completed.

While Deputy Lane was intent on getting the blood alcohol results, he was also interested in the suicide test, as if it might reveal something even more nefarious about the couple than he first thought. He gave the nurses his blessing to proceed, as if they needed it.

Lane wondered if it was possible to obtain the results of the suicide tests, thinking that, if he could get his hands on them, it would bolster his belief that Jack and Aria had been lying to him—that they hadn't fallen off the bridge accidentally. And if that were true, even if he wasn't exactly sure what he could or would do with the information, he at least would find some satisfaction in knowing he had been right all along.

Lane again approached the nurses after they exited the respective exam rooms.

"So, what do you think?"

Nurse Rita frowned up at the tall Deputy.

"Well, if you must know, we've referred them to our psych nurses for more evaluation. Does that make you happy?"

Deputy Lane ignored Nurse Rita's challenge and moved on to his other interest.

"How about the blood tests?"

"Those are next. We have to track down the phlebotomist."

Deputy Lane had no idea what a phlebotomist did, or even how to spell "phlebotomist," but wasn't about to let the nurses know that. He'd already been forced to ask them what CSSRS meant and they didn't seem to like it when he questioned them on *any* topic.

"Uh, okay. Yeah, of course. Sounds good. Thank you."

Lane watched the nurses walk away and, feeling a tad cranky, returned to his spot on the far wall, wishing he had been the one to administer the tests.

*How hard can it be to read questions off a sheet of paper? Besides, I had to take Psych 101. I bet I could give that test as good as anyone here.*

Deputy Lane watched as a man in a lab coat entered Jack's room and wondered if he was the flegotamist, or however it was pronounced. He looked at his watch. He wasn't sure how long it took to get blood test results, but promised himself he wasn't leaving until they arrived.

Gary the phlebotomist had just come from exam room seven, where he had taken blood from the arm of a friendly priest with a slight Irish accent. Gary was Catholic and would never have called a priest by his first name, but Father O'Neal insisted no less than three times that Gary call him Randall. Finally, Gary complied and the two had a nice chat about the snowstorm and all the people who had ended up in the emergency room as a result of the unexpected weather.

Gary's assignment was simply to remove, from the priest's arm, a sufficient amount of blood to perform a blood alcohol test, a task he was also going to undertake with two more patients as soon as he was finished with Father O'Neal . . . Randall.

Gary was an experienced phlebotomist, and the whole thing should have taken less than three minutes, but he found the priest charming and amiable, and lingered for at least ten minutes while they chatted. He would have dawdled further had their conversation not been interrupted by Nurse Rita Dolworth.

"Can you please get over there to 9 and 10? That cop's still hanging around and I want to get rid of him."

She turned but looked back over her shoulder.

"Sorry to interrupt, Father."

Gary made his goodbyes to Father Randall and did as requested, packing up his gear and making his way to Exam Room 9 which, according to Nurse Rita and the chart hanging in the room, was occupied by a man named Jack Current. The new patient was wearing scrubs, which initially threw Gary, who expected all patients to be in hospital gowns, if not the clothes in which they arrived.

"Hi, Jack. I'm Gary. I'm here to take some blood for a blood alcohol test. Did they let you know I'd be coming?"

Jack nodded.

"They did. I'm getting all kinds of tests tonight."

Gary smiled as he readied his blood-removal paraphernalia.

"Well, mine's easy and quick. Promise."

Seeing as how the night had gone so far, Jack doubted the promise would be kept, but saw no reason to object.

Aria was aware of Gary's arrival. When the nurses left, she had every intention of sneaking back into Jack's room so she could see how he was doing, but decided to wait a minute and see if anybody else walked back in. She relayed this strategy to Jack, who agreed it was wise to wait and see.

The waiting paid off when Gary entered Jack's exam room on the heels of the departed nurses.

But Aria decided she wasn't going to let a vampire in a lab coat stop her from seeing Jack, and she slipped around the curtain just in time to see Gary sliding a needle into Jack's arm.

Aria did not like needles, and seeing one poke into Jack's arm made her woozy. As a high school student, she'd twice played the role of mad surgeon at the Haunted School House, but that was fake blood. Real blood made her faint, something she learned the first time she volunteered at the blood bank. In this case she did not pass out.

Gary finished with Jack before turning to Aria with a smile. "I believe you're next."

Aria's blood draw went off without a hitch, and Gary left with his samples and gear, leaving the couple sitting together on the bed. For a minute they just looked at each other, pleased by their physical proximity and each wondering what they might be able to orchestrate on a bed in the middle of a busy emergency room. Wordlessly, they realized the answer to the question was nothing. There was no time and too much activity going on around them.

But, on an impulse, Aria turned away from Jack and, while humming a burlesque tune—da-da-dun, da-da-da-dun—slowly lifted her scrub blouse to her shoulders, exposing her bare back to him. She flashed him a smile over her shoulder before letting the blouse drop back down to her waist. The teasing rendered Jack speechless, but his eyes were drawn to a long purple bruise on her back. It looked like she'd been caned.

"Ooh, Aria. Does that hurt?"

"Does what hurt?"

"You have a big bruise on your lower back."

"Hmm. I didn't notice. No, it doesn't really hurt. I guess I kinda hurt all over. We're both pretty bruised up. I'm sure I'll get to see one of yourd before long." She smiled, her eyes giving him a quick once-over.

Her none-too-subtle flirtation continued to fluster Jack. Aria, undeterred, was on a roll.

She raised her eyebrows questioningly and waved her hand over the bed. "Do we just stay in here?"

"Um . . . I think so?"

In light of Aria's suggestion of future nudity and a shared bed, Jack was having a problem concentrating on post-bloodwork procedure. He was saved by the appearance of Nurse Rita Dolworth, who'd entered silently, and without moving any of the curtains, not unlike a ninja assassin.

"Alright you two, I'm sending you upstairs, to the fourth floor. Here, take this."

Nurse Rita handed a file folder to Jack.

"Give that to whoever checks you in and they'll take it from there. Understand?"

Jack and Aria nodded, their carnal imaginings crushed, for the moment, by the straightforward instructions of Nurse Rita, who turned and walked out of the exam room. But her voice filtered in through the curtain.

"Now, please."

Aria was disappointed. "What? No wheelchair this time?"

Nurse Rita heard the complaint. "Too busy. You'll be fine."

Jack and Aria gave each other, and then the bed, a look of longing and regret as they left the exam room, their exit observed by Deputy Lane, who abandoned his spot on the wall to intercept the young couple before they made it to the elevators.

"Where are you two headed?"

*To a little place called "None of Your Damned Business"* was what Jack was tempted to say, but thought better of it. Aria, however, did not hold her tongue.

"Upstairs. They told us to go up to the fourth floor to talk to a psych nurse."

She paused, then continued very seriously.

"Did you want to go with us? I'm sure they could make time for you."

Jack allowed a small laugh to escape but Deputy Lane chose to ignore Aria's sarcasm, as well as Jack's reaction to it.

"I'll be waiting for the results of your blood tests. We'll talk again."

"Oooh, sounds scary. What are you going to do? Arrest us for drunk walking?"

"No, Miss Balfour. That's not necessarily illegal, but jumping off the bridge is. So, go check on your sanity test and we'll just see."

Aria grabbed Jack's hand, pulled him away from Deputy Lane, and led him toward the elevator. Jack was happy to have her take the lead, but needed to return to his exam room before they headed upstairs.

"Give me just a sec."

He let go of Aria's hand, ducked into his exam room and emerged with the notebook he'd obtained earlier from the gift shop.

"We might need this."

Aria had no idea what he meant but was happy he wanted to bring the pad with them. He clearly wanted to keep writing. She, however, did not feel the urge to grab the little notebook, and told herself she would use it later.

Aria took Jack's hand back into her own and gave him a little tug.

"Let's get this over with."

The elevator moved at a snail's pace, which Jack assumed was by design. After all, they were in a hospital, where a good percentage of people riding it might be unstable.

*At least physically.*

# Chapter Twelve

## Love and Other Drugs

The elevator doors opened to a hallway, which separated them from an empty, noiseless space, populated only by chairs, another intake desk, and a water fountain, none of which were currently in use. The emptiness of the waiting room caused Jack and Aria to hesitate, and they lingered in the elevator until the doors began to close again, prompting Jack to thrust his arm between them. They stepped out of the elevator once the doors reversed direction.

Aria giggled. "I think I see some open seats in the corner."

"Let's hurry before someone else gets them."

They were actually thrilled to find the room empty. They'd grown tired of the exam rooms in the bustling emergency department, where they'd been constantly interrupted by hospital staff. And they were tired as well of the watchful eye of Deputy Lane. The empty waiting room afforded them an opportunity to relax, to take a breath.

They examined the intake desk and located no buzzer or bell to announce their presence to the powers that be. So they sat down, assuming they were being monitored by a hidden camera. Neither, however, performed more than a cursory attempt to locate the camera itself.

Aria sighed. "They've got to know we're here, right?"

"Right. I'm sure Nurse Rita sent word, or something, to let them know we were coming. Let's give it a few minutes, and if no one comes out I'll knock on that door behind the desk."

Jack motioned to the door in question.

"I figure that's where they keep the doctors and nurses."

Aria giggled again.

"Or maybe the crazy people."

"Then we're in the right place."

Aria fidgeted, shifting this way and that in an attempt to find a comfortable position. Jack looked around for an opportunity to help her, grabbed two armless chairs and dragged them over to where they were sitting. He lined them up in a row in front of Aria.

"Do you want to lie down on these?"

"Oh, hell yes. Thank you so much, Jack."

Aria unfolded her legs, shifted her midsection to the second chair and found a position that didn't put too much pressure on her bruises. She made herself comfortable, and before long she was dozing.

Jack remained seated, thinking one of them needed to stand guard should the as-yet-to-be-seen psych nurses suddenly make themselves known. Jack didn't think it was a problem to be found sleeping in the waiting room, but didn't want to get taken by surprise, so he decided to watch over Aria while she slept.

It wasn't long, however, before the quiet, dimly lit room began to have the same effect on Jack as it was having on Aria and, after the third time he caught himself nodding off, figured he needed something to help him stay awake. Coffee wasn't out of the question, but the trip presented two problems, the first being he would have to leave Aria alone. The second was that he couldn't remember exactly where the vending machines were located, the ones Harvey had told him about in the gift shop. He still had the money Harvey had given him, but no idea where to go to use it.

In similar low-key situations, Jack would have taken the opportunity to play games on his phone, but he didn't have his phone. It was sitting on a counter in his apartment, waiting to be discovered after his death. His normal distractions unavailable, Jack decided this was a good opportunity to write in the log, which he'd wisely brought with him from the emergency room.

*5:32 AM*

*Jeez, is it really 5:32 in the morning? What the hell is going on?*

*Well, I know what's going on, mostly, I think.*

*I'm sure there's parts I'm not really sure about, like what the hell Deputy Lane is up to.*

*Or, for that matter, exactly what is happening between Aria and me.*

*I mean, there's definitely something happening, I'm just not sure what to name it.*

*If I think about it (and I have been thinking about it) I want whatever is happening to happen, whatever that may be.*

*And I hope...well, okay, I believe she wants it to happen too. All signs point to that.*

*I will say something to her, ask her about it, when I get the chance.*

*I'm sure as hell not going to wake her up to ask her where we stand in our relationship.*

*Would she even know?*

*This is exactly the kind of conversation I've never been good at.*

*But, I think, honestly, is there anything I can't say to her at this point?*

*I think we've earned the trust, or the intimacy, or whatever you want to call it.*

*Like I said, I'll talk to her when the time is right.*

*Now I think I'm going to go look for some coffee.*

Jack turned to the next blank page, tore it out as gently so as not to wake Aria.

**IN CASE YOU WAKE UP BEFORE I GET BACK – I'M GET-TING US COFFEE. I HAVE TO LEAVE YOU ALONE FOR A FEW MINUTES, EVEN THOUGH I DON'T WANT TO.**

Jack stood and left the note on his chair, hoping it was the first thing Aria would see if she woke up. He strode into the hallway looking for directional signs, but discovered none specifically indicating the way to a coffee vending machine. One sign, however, did point in the direction of a breakroom. It did not indicate what, exactly, was available to be consumed in the breakroom, only that it existed, and that it was on the same floor as Jack, Aria, and the empty waiting room. Harboring no desire to go back to the first floor, Jack followed the arrow, hoping for coffee at the end of his rainbow.

Aria woke within a minute of Jack leaving her side. No noise or movement was responsible for waking her, rather the waking was caused by the *lack* of something. Of course, that something was Jack, though she didn't know it. Upon opening her eyes after five minutes of dozing, and being confronted by the same dim lighting and empti-ness, Aria experienced an acute moment of anxiousness. But her uneasiness dissipated after finding his note.

*Oh my God, coffee sounds perfect. Thank you, Jack.*

Jack had left the notebook and pen laying underneath the coffee message, so she sat up in one of her chairs, grabbed the pad and considered what to do. She wondered, as she had in the bar hours and hours earlier, what he'd been writing. But, like before, she was confronted with the ethical issue that taking a peek inside Jack's private writing would entail. After a few moments of indecision, she reminded herself Jack had actually written directly to her on the pages themselves. This made it easy to make the same choice she'd made in the bar and earlier in the emergency room: She cracked open the notebook and read his last entry.

Jack's words pierced her heart. It wasn't Shakespeare, but she was nonetheless moved. She was exhausted and her emotions raw. After the twists and turns and ups and downs of the last twelve hours, tears were the natural reaction to his words—fighting them back, nonetheless, she decided to respond and hoped he would understand.

Even more, she hoped he would like it.

*5:38 AM*

*Okay, so I hope this is okay, Jack. Writing in your log and all. I know you gave me that notebook to write in, and I actually did write in it, but I think I left it in the exam room.*

*You're out looking for coffee right now. I can't tell you how excited I am about the chance you might be bringing some back here for us. I don't think I've ever been so tired in my life. Right now, I can't really remember, but I think that's true. It doesn't matter, though. Coffee! Yay!*

*Something else... I read the log again. This one – the one I'm writing in right now. I don't know why I keep reading them. It's a compulsion. In a way I feel bad about it because it's personal, but now I think you want me to read it, and when I think about that, I don't feel bad at all. Me reading what you wrote in your notebook led me to you on the bridge. It led us here tonight, to this ridiculous situation in this ridiculous,*

148

*empty waiting room. So, yeah, I guess I don't feel bad about it.*

*Did I mention this has been the best night of my life. Surprised?*

*Yup, even with the near-death experience, or maybe because of it, plus everything else that's happened (so far.) I mean, who gets to do all this stuff? It's really incredible if you think about it.*

*Which leads me to what you wrote. The part you just wrote, I think, before you went to get coffee.*

*I want whatever is happening between us to happen, too. Honestly, I don't think we can stop it.*

*It's happening already (see above where I talk about what an amazing night we're having.)*

*And if it's happening already, then I know we'll just keep taking it as it comes.*

*So, yes. Yes to you and me. Yes to everything that has happened. Yes to what is going to happen.*

*Hold on – I think you're coming back. If you've got coffee I'm*

*going to love you forever.*

*But not in a crazy, stalker way.*


Jack walked carefully down the passageway, working hard not to spill the two cups of coffee he'd snagged in the breakroom. The signs led him there, just as he'd hoped, and he was more than pleasantly surprised to find it contained the requisite vending equipment. He felt doubly lucky for the three dollars Harvey had given him, a dollar more than he needed for two cups of hot java.

Luckily, what the staff break room lacked, was staff. It was as barren as the psych nurse waiting room, although the lighting was better. Jack had spotted not a soul on his journey to coffee heaven, and was beginning to think he and Aria might be the only people on the entire floor. Granted, his exploration of the fourth floor had thus far been minimal, focused on the two rooms in which he'd spent any time. And that was just fine with Jack. He felt other humans would merely be a distraction to his coffee mission. Even worse, they might have emptied the machine. But the best thing about the trip, he thought—other than the coffee—was that this time he did *not* run into the hospital security guard.

Jack wasn't sure how Aria took her coffee, and bought two: one with cream and one with cream and sugar. He considered using his last dollar to purchase a plain, black coffee, but the thought of carrying three open containers of burning liquid back to the waiting room without spilling was daunting, and besides, he might need that dollar for something else.

Aria was awake when Jack returned. She was sitting up in a chair and, when she saw Jack was successful in his hunt, gave him a gentle round of applause. She would have clapped louder but didn't want to disturb any ghosts in the room.

"Do you want cream? Or cream and sugar?"

"Cream and sugar, please."

"Thank, God. I was afraid you'd want yours black."

Jack handed Aria one of the cups and sat down next to her.

"So, anything interesting happen while I was gone? Did any nurses miraculously appear?"

"Nope. I was alone the whole time. I think I woke up right after you left."

Aria decided not to mention she'd been writing in the log, figuring she could do that later, after she was done fortifying herself with caffeine. Besides, it was likely Jack would just find her words in there anyway, and then either be happy, or unhappy; she was pretty sure "indifferent" was not on the table. She would have preferred "happy," but would cross that bridge when she came to it.

"What about you?" Aria nudged Jack with her elbow, careful not to make him spill. "Tell me about the fourth floor. Any dead people laying around? Oooh! Any zombies?"

Jack laughed with her.

"Nope, no dead people or zombies as far as I could tell. But I may have missed something. I was very focused on finding the coffee."

He took a sip from his cup. "I did see a sign for the pharmacy, though."

"Pharmacy?"

"Yup. The sign said it was on the first floor."

Aria smiled over her coffee. "Are you having some sort of idea about the pharmacy?"

"Well, yeah, I guess. I was just thinking ..."

"Thinking what?"

"I was just thinking, you know, we're tired. I'm tired. We've been awake for close to 24 hours, and it's not over yet. Maybe there'd be something in the pharmacy that could help us out."

"And you're okay with going back down to the first floor? Look around, Jack."

Aria made a sweeping motion with her left arm.

"We've got it good up here. Nobody's bugging us. No more sui-cide tests. No blood tests. No threats about a three-day confinement in "Bellevue," or whatever they call it here. You sure you want to give all this up?"

Jack thought for a moment.

"Unfortunately, I think we have to, Aria. They might come out that door at any time. I mean, as of now we've managed to piss off the cops *and* the hospital. I'm not sure how it's going to play out."

Aria smiled again. "And how does a trip to the pharmacy play into all this?"

"Good question. Not really sure, except that I don't want to go back to the emergency room, and I don't think the coffee is going to be enough to keep us sharp. Who knows what they'll throw at us next?"

"Good point. But what if the pharmacy is closed, or manned, or whatever?"

Aria knew Jack was right, that the psych nurse could appear at any time. She was in no mood to answer any more questions about her sister, her life, and any "suicidal thoughts" she may or may not have. She figured it was ok to take their chances back on the first floor, as long as they could avoid the emergency room and Deputy Lane, although she really did want to recover the teddy bear.

"Alright, Jack. Let's go for it, but we're taking the coffee with us."

"Absolutely."

"And I want my teddy bear." Aria frowned. "Did I thank you for the bear?"

"I don't remember, but you're welcome."

Jack smiled as they moved the chairs back to their original spots and walked out of the room. He grabbed the notebook as they left, carrying it in one hand and his coffee in the other. Aria, who still had a free hand, hit the down button on the elevator.

"Which way do we go when we get off the elevator?"

Jack thought about it while he took a sip.

"Left, I think. Right takes us to the ER. We don't want to go that way. Not yet, anyway."

Aria smiled. In spite of everything, she was having fun sneaking around the hospital with Jack.

*Best night ever.*

When the elevator doors opened to the first floor, Aria followed Jack out and they turned down the hallway, away from the emergency room. The pharmacy was surprisingly close, looming before them less than a minute after leaving the elevator. They slowed their pace as they approached the doorway, which was split in half, farmhouse style. This was not a public pharmacy—no sundries, no health and beauty aids, no candy, no greeting cards—only drugs.

The top half of the door was open, giving them a good view of the interior. Peeking inside, they could see a man in a white lab coat slumped over at one of the computer stations, sleeping, perhaps. Or dead. As far as they could tell, he was the only person in the room. Aria looked up and down the first-floor hallway to make sure the coast was clear and nodded at Jack, who gently turned the doorknob so as not to wake the dead man slumped over the computer keyboard.

They opened the bottom half of the door and strode into the room, somehow less fearful of getting caught stealing drugs than of getting arrested for drunk bridge jumping. The room was not as large as either of them expected though, admittedly, neither had any experience with hospital pharmacies. Jack signaled, as best he could, that they should explore the aisles and see if there was anything they might find useful. Aria started with the first row while Jack tiptoed to the last, past the sagging pharmacist. In passing, Jack glanced at the computer screen, now filled with the letter Z, the key on which one of the pharmacist's elbows rested.

The vast array of drugs lining the shelves was dizzying and, as far as Jack could tell, the various pharmacological offerings were not listed alphabetically. His drug of choice had always been alcohol, and he had little to no experience with most of the products being churned out by the pharmaceutical industry. He was hoping to find something he knew would keep them awake, like Ritalin, but either there was none in stock, it was listed under another name, or he missed the bottle, an easy thing to do given the monotonous sameness of the packaging.

Jack did have one success, however. While scanning for drugs that would keep them awake, he spotted a rather large bottle of Oxycodone. He grabbed it and stuffed it into the pocket of his scrubs. His hip had been bothering him on and off all morning, but knowing he had the painkillers somehow made it feel better, even though he didn't immediately ingest any of the pills.

Aria was having the same problem as Jack when it came to finding the right wake-me-up drug, although her knowledge of psychotropics was a tad more extensive than his. As they tiptoed up and down the aisles, they searched but found nothing that described what effects any of the drugs might have. Given the miniscule writing on the bottles, they couldn't be sure if they were reading instructions or warnings, and they had to be careful not to take anything that would turn them purple or cause permanent damage to their reproductive systems or other important organs.

Having started from opposite ends of the room, they ended up meeting in the middle aisle, disappointed with the results of their search.

Aria put her hands on Jack's shoulders and pulled herself up on her tiptoes so he could hear the whisper. "I didn't see anything I was sure about."

"Me neither. Well, except these."

Aria viewed the large bottle of painkillers in amazement.

"Holy crap! I don't think we need that many."

"Good point." Jack removed the bottle top, poured a handful of pills into his pocket and left the bottle on the closest shelf.

They were ready to give up on their plan to steal (more) drugs when the pharmacy telephone started to ring. Anxious to exit before the pharmacist woke from his slobbery slumber, Aria randomly snagged one of the smallish bottles off a shelf, grabbed Jack's hand and pulled him out the door.

As it turned out, they'd run for no reason. The ringer failed to wake the sleepy drug dealer. Jack and Aria were safe, though they didn't know it as they ran down the hallway, finally pausing in front of the door to a supply closet.

"What'd you get?"

Aria held the bottle up for examination.

"Modafinil? Any idea what it does?"

Jack thought for a moment.

"Wait, I think that's a drug for narcolepsy. You know, that thing where you just, sort of, randomly pass out? One of the guys at work took it for that. Kept him from crashing his head on his desk. You might have lucked out and grabbed something that won't kill us."

"You want one?"

"I'm in if you are. I'm going to take one of these, too." Jack patted the Oxycodone bulge in his pocket and looked around.

"But let's get out of this hallway. I feel naked out here."

Aria tried the handle of the supply closet. It was not locked and yielded easily to her pressure. As she and Jack slipped inside, the wall sensor brightened the overhead light. They sat on the floor, resting their backs against the only stretch of wall not covered by shelving.

Jack winced as his injured hip settled into place, the adrenaline from the drug heist already beginning to subside. Aria unscrewed the top of her bottle.

"One for you ..."

She handed Jack a pill.

". . . and one for me."

Jack reached into his pocket and pulled out a few of the oxyco-done pills.

"Do you want one of these? They really do help with the pain."

"I'm good for now, but don't lose those."

Jack kept one for himself and put the rest back in his pocket.

"Bottoms up."

Jack and Aria popped their pills, chased them with coffee, and waited for the effects to kick in. The closet was surprisingly spacious and contained all manner of useful consumable products. They leaned back, admired the vast amounts of toilet paper, hand soap, and spare sheets, and took the opportunity to stretch their legs in front of them, which forced the notebook out of Jack's pocket. He picked it up and was about to open it when Aria spoke.

"Jack, um, I hope you don't mind, but I read your notebook earlier. Oh, and I also wrote in your notebook."

"Really? When did you have the chance to do that?"

"When you went to get coffee. I woke up when you left the room and saw the notebook sitting there and, well, I guess I wanted to see what you were writing about, and when I did read it, I just thought . . . I felt like I wanted you to know how I felt, too. So, I wrote back to you."

Jack was unperturbed. "Can I read it?"

"Of course."

Perceiving no discernable movement, the sensor dimmed the closet light. Even so, Jack had no problem reading Aria's words and, when he finished her entry, couldn't take his eyes off the page, amazed at how good it felt to see her words in the log, next to his.

"Is it okay?"

Jack set the notebook down and stared at her.

"It's perfect. It's beautiful. I want more."

Aria wasn't sure how to respond, so she put her hands behind Jack's head, entangling her fingers in his hair, and pulled his face down to hers.

The kissing, at first, was enough. Other than the brief kiss for luck he'd received before his notebook-hunting expedition, it had been months and months since they had kissed each other, months and months since Jack and Aria had kissed anyone. At first, it was enough.

Jack knew it was okay to touch her. He knew it was ok to touch her when she touched him, when her hand slid under his scrubs. It started on his stomach, worked its way to his back, and then she pulled his body toward hers.

Jack allowed her to pull him down. It was easy to let her. It was the easiest thing he'd ever done. They felt the thrill of discovery as each removed the other's clothes and their urgency triggered the light sensor. Now their bodies, blemished by the debris of a turbulent, freezing river, lay naked and exposed to each other on the floor of a hospital storage closet, as exposed as their words on the page of the notebook.

Harvey found them. He needed a bottle of spray cleaner, having identified a trail of coffee dripped down the hallway, and found them lying in a nest of hospital sheets, towels and scrubs, using rolls of paper towels as pillows and spooning on the floor. They were awake, the Modafinil having kicked in soon after it hit their stomachs.

Harvey didn't know anything about Modafinil, but he did know something about human relations. He slipped into the closet, being careful to avert his eyes from the naked couple on the floor, pretending not to notice them. But he did notice them.

"If you two will excuse me, I just need a bottle of Lysol. And I'll take one of those rolls of paper towels, if you don't mind."

# Chapter Thirteen

## Fifty Shades of Black and Blue

Harvey's entrance had triggered the lights. They'd dimmed after
Jack and Aria stopped moving but, again brightened, forced everyone's eyes to adjust. The entire room and its contents, human and
otherwise, were naked to the human eye. Jack looked up at the
maintenance man through squinted lids, recognizing him as the man
who'd helped him in the gift shop.

"Oh, hi Harvey."

Jack greeted him like an old friend, but his voice revealed some
embarrassment, as he and Aria were (mostly) in a state of undress,
and had somehow managed to ignore the fact there was no lock on the
door. By the time Harvey walked in they were basking in the after-
glow, spooning under a mix of sheets and towels. Luckily for them
and Harvey, the materials they used to fashion their love nest sufficiently covered their vital areas.

Harvey, having averted his eyes, did not immediately recognize
Jack. However, once addressed directly, he was forced to look at the
semi-clad lovers, lest he appear rude, which was not in his character.

"Well, hello there, young man and young lady. It's Jack, right?"

Harvey had never been good at remembering names, but his contact with Jack thus far had been unique, and therefore easily recalled.

"Yessir."

Jack wasn't sure what to say.

"I'm sorry about this, Harvey. We were, well, we *are* kind of hiding, and we ducked in here, and then ..."

Harvey gently interrupted.

"That's fine, Jack. You don't need to tell me everything, and I don't need to know everything. I've been working here a long time, and very little surprises me anymore. I'll just go about my business and be on my way."

"Thank you, Harvey. I'm Aria, by the way."

Until then, Aria had said nothing, supporting Jack by simply nodding in agreement when the moment seemed to call for it.

"I promise we won't be here much longer. All we really want to do is get home."

Harvey sighed, still attempting not to look directly at Jack and Aria, but unable to completely ignore the pile of laundry they'd soiled.

"I understand how that feels, Aria. So, listen, I want you both to understand something. I'm not the only one with access to this closet. People are in and out of here all the time. The longer you stay, the more chance you have of getting caught. You've gotten lucky because it's been a slow morning."

"Jeez, it is morning, isn't it?" Jack almost whispered the words but they seemed to amplify as they bounced off bottles of hand sanitizer and toilet bowl cleaner.

"Morning it is, young man, and my shift ends soon. I guarantee things will start picking up in the next hour or so, when the day shift starts comin' in. I don't know how they'll feel about the two of you hiding in here, so you'll want to be out before then. Understand?"

Aria and Jack nodded.

"Alright, then. Well, I'm going to go finish up out there and, just so you know, if I was trying to sneak out of this hospital, I'd try the hall that runs past the chapel. It's pretty quiet over there."

"Thank you, Harvey."

"You're welcome, Jack."

Harvey opened the door gently so as not to bounce it off Jack or Aria, but also to avoid drawing attention, and whisked himself out.

Jack and Aria were again alone in the storage closet, but Harvey's entrance and exit had broken whatever magic they had created among the rows of bleach and toilet brushes, at least for the moment. The door gently closed itself, leaving Jack and Aria sitting in their nest, wondering about the conversation they just had with the janitor.

"Maybe we should ..."

"Yeah, let's get dressed."

Though they'd just spent a considerable amount of time examining each other's bodies with eyes, hands, and lips, Jack and Aria, out of habit, turned away from each other and swiftly re-robed. The whole process took less than a minute.

Jack turned back to Aria. "Um, what do you think about more coffee? I've got enough money for one more cup. We could share."

"Oh, yes, please. Coffee sounds great. Do you think you can get there and back without anything weird happening, you know, with the cops or security?"

Aria didn't really want, or need, any more coffee. For that matter, neither did Jack. Their stomachs were empty and the modafinil was doing its job, but they needed a way to escape the awkward moment in which they had found themselves, and a coffee hunt was as good an excuse as any.

Jack stood up, feeling the extra strain in his hip from his recent activity—a repetitive motion he had not experienced in a very long time—but a strain, and a pain, he would not have foregone for the world. He decided this was a good time to take another Oxycodone and pulled a couple out of his pocket.

"Care for one now?"

161

"Yeah, I'll take one. I'm feeling sore." Aria reached out and touched his leg. "Are you going to be ok?"

"I think I'll be good. Really."

He touched his temple with his left index finger.

"I've got the route down pat. Be right back."

Jack cracked open the door and peered out, checking to make sure the coast was clear. He stopped to look down at Aria and give her a little wave before squishing himself through the door opening and into the hallway.

Jack's exit, as had Harvey's, bathed Aria in an annoying level of illumination. But instead of reaching up and tapping the manual part of the light switch, she decided instead to sit as still as possible, faking out the miracle of modern technology until the sensor dimmed the lights accordingly.

Aria wasn't sure how long this would take so she waited, biding her time looking around the room, counting towel piles, reciting the names of various cleaners, and generally just keeping herself busy in any way she could, short of actually moving. Finally, the lights dimmed.

Aria spied Jack's notebook on the floor where he had been sitting, the pen in its wire spine, and wondered if Jack had written in it after she did. She wanted to check, felt she *needed* to check, but did not want to activate the light sensor. This had become a game she was playing with herself—one she didn't want to lose. So, ever so slowly, she slid her hand across the floor until her fingers touched the edge of the pad. Then, as carefully as she could, slid the notebook, inch by inch, back toward her leg. Barely breathing, she picked it up and placed it on her lap.

Aria cautiously opened the notebook, pleased she'd not triggered the sensor. Even in the dim light, she could see that Jack hadn't written anything more. She found this disappointing, even as she realized he'd hardly had the time, given all that had happened since he brought her that first cup of coffee—the one that would decide if she loved him forever, or not. She wondered, having now declared her love in writing, what token of her emotional self she could offer in return for the gift of a second cup.

*6:15 (maybe)*
*I'm guessing at the time. There's no clock in here. I'll look for one when I get out of this closet.*
*So, you're off getting me another cup of coffee. I don't know if you noticed, but on the page behind this one I promised you my undying love if you brought me coffee. And then you did. So, yeah, you've got my undying love. Is there anything else I can do for you? (Other than that thing I did for you a little bit ago that we both seemed to like?) Seriously, though, I've been trying to think of something I could give you, like you gave me the teddy bear, for the coffee you're getting us right now. Problem is, at this point, all I have to give you is undying love. All my other stuff is in a plastic bag in the emergency room. I suppose I could give you a piece of my clothing (panties?), Eww! Scratch that. Well, maybe . . . after I wash everything.*
*Okay, I'm going to check the time now. Wish me luck.*

Aria flipped to her knees, activating the sensor, reached up to turn the door handle and peeked out into the hallway. As far as she could tell, it was empty, which was good, but she couldn't see a clock, which was bad. To find a clock, she would have to venture out from the safety of the supply closet and into the unknown.

163

*There's got to be a clock close by. This place is sick with them.*

Aria stood and opened the door just wide enough to slip into the empty hallway, turned in the direction opposite the pharmacy and started walking. Head up and shoulders back, she wanted to look like she belonged, at least to the casual observer. A clipboard would have completed the illusion. The socks helped her move quietly, but would give her away if noticed.

Aria didn't have to go far to locate a wall clock. She traveled no more than twenty steps when she spotted it. 6:12. She repeated it in her head a few times to make sure she remembered and smiled at how closely she guessed the time in the log, but as she turned to make her way back to the storage closet, a door opened and closed behind her and another nurse, a real one, came at her from the opposite direction.

"Are you busy?"

*Is she talking to me?*

The real nurse seemed in a rush.

*Holy crap. She's talking to me.*

"Um, no?"

Aria knew it was the wrong answer, even though it was the truth.

"Okay, listen, I need you down to 12. Mr. Ross is in danger of coding, and I need to go to the pharmacy to get some Klonopin. Can you keep an eye on him for a few minutes?"

The real nurse, clearly preoccupied, hadn't the time to notice Aria's eclectic choice of hair style and footwear or, for that matter, her lack of a legitimate hospital badge and basic nursing accessories, like a stethoscope.

Aria was between a rock and hard place. Neither her formal education nor her time spent tending bar at Liberty's had done anything to prepare her for this moment and the only reason she knew the meaning of "code" in medical parlance was from countless hours spent watching Grey's Anatomy reruns.

"Okay," she said. "How long will you be?"

"Just a few minutes," said the real nurse. "Stay with him and keep an eye on his vitals."

The real nurse sprinted past Aria toward the pharmacy while Aria walked at a quickened pace to where she suspected, correctly, Room 12 to be located. Sheepishly, she cracked the door open to find an old man on a bed, a plethora of tubes and wires running from his body to various machines. To her surprise, Aria recognized at least one of them. The heart monitor beeped rapidly, indicating a heart rate closing in on 132 beats per minute. His blood pressure was 212 over 102. Aria didn't know what either number stood for but figured if the man's nurse was in a big rush to get him some drugs, then they couldn't stand for anything good.

Aria made her way through the forest of equipment to the side of the bed. Initially, the old man appeared to be sleeping, but when Aria accidentally knocked one machine into the one next to it, he opened his eyes.

"I think I'm ready, nurse."

"What? Ready for what?"

Aria's own heart rate started to rise.

*What the hell is happening?*

"Ready to let go."

The man's voice squeaked out of his mouth as a hoarse whisper, but Aria was now sure what he was saying.

"Oh, God, no you're not, sir. Don't say that. Let's just wait for the other nurse to get back before you do anything, okay? Don't let go. Don't go into the light!"

Aria was in a panic, questioning the choice she made in the hallway, and wondering if she should just run out of the room and escape back to the closet. Instead, she took Mr. Ross' hand in her own, giving it a gentle squeeze. He returned the squeeze before his hand went slack.

*Flatline.*

That was another word Aria had learned from medical dramas.

As the heart monitor switched from a rhythmic beep to a low, mechanical hum, the real nurse rushed back into the room.

"Start chest compressions."

*What? Start what?*

It took a few seconds, but Aria's lifeguard CPR training started to guide her actions as she worked opposite the real nurse. She was proud of herself for doing it correctly. At least she thought she was doing it correctly. She didn't hear any bones cracking, and it only took her four compressions to bring Mr. Ross back to life. The unexpected draw of his life's breath nearly startled her out of her socks.

"Okay, stop compressions. Good job."

The real nurse was all business.

"Do you need me for anything else?"

Aria couldn't believe she'd even asked the question. She still had no idea how she had actually saved the man's life.

*I'm not even wearing shoes!*

The real nurse didn't look up from Mr. Ross. "No, I'm good. Thanks again. I'll come get you if I need you."

*That would be an incredibly bad idea.*

Aria backed out of the room, breathless, and gently sped back to the storage closet, noting the new time on the wall clock and vowing not to leave the closet again for any reason except a bathroom trip.

The light activated upon her reentry, and Aria stood amongst the brightly lit shelves for a minute to allow her breathing to steady. When it did, she grabbed the notebook and sat down.

*6:19 AM*

*You're not going to believe what just happened! Where do I start?*

*Okay, – I went out in the hallway to check the time and ended up saving someone's life.*

*Not kidding. This nurse who needed help saw me in the hallway and thought I was a real nurse, like her. I ended up watching her patient while she went to get something from the pharmacy, and then the old guy died. That's when the nurse came back and tells me to do CPR—WHICH I DO! And before I knew it, he came back to life. It was incredible.*

*You know what? Maybe I should become a doctor or a nurse. Maybe that's what I should have done instead of that stupid*

*business degree. I'll think about it.*

*I mean, the whole thing was crazy. Exciting.*

*I wonder if he died again after I left. And I wonder if that's actually what he really wanted. So maybe I'm okay with that. Maybe sometimes it's okay to want to die. Maybe sometimes it's not.*

Aria put the pad down just as the door opened and Jack entered, holding a single cup of coffee. He was careful not to spill as he sat down on the floor.

"I hope it's okay. I went to the same machine as last time."

Jack handed Aria the coffee and she took a sip. It was as good as the last time. Maybe better. She wondered if she should reveal her undying love for him, thinking she might need to drink something stronger than coffee before she had that kind of courage and forgetting she had already committed the words to paper.

"It's good. Thanks, Jack. Anything interesting happen while you were sneaking around the hospital?"

She really was interested in Jack's travels but was a bit desperate for him to ask her the same.

"Nope. Clear sailing, except I spent a lot of time backtracking, hiding, and sneaking around to avoid running into anyone. How about you? Anything interesting happen while I was gone?"

Aria proceeded to tell Jack about how she got caught in the hallway, agreed to watch a dying patient while his nurse ran to the pharmacy, and how she saved his life. She did not mention her newfound interest in medical school.

"Jeez, Aria. I go to get a cup of coffee and, while I'm gone, you bring someone back from the dead? Your time was definitely spent better than mine. Let me know if it happens again. I'd like to be there."

"I'll try to make sure you're around for the next time." She smiled wryly, but the allusion seemed to be lost on Jack.

*Third time's a charm?*

Aria handed the coffee back to Jack. He took a drink while she pondered their next move.

"Any ideas on what we should do next? I mean, we can't stay in this closet forever, but I think we have a little time, at least according to Harvey. Even so, we should probably get out of here soon."

"How soon?"

Jack passed the coffee back to Aria.

168

"I don't know. At least before seven, I think."

"Okay, how do you want to kill time until we go?"

"More sex?" Aria suggested hopefully.

Jack did not dismiss the idea out of hand, but was distracted by the chance of Harvey's daytime counterpart walking in on them.

"I can't tell you how much I hate saying this, but not more sex. At least not right now."

Aria pulled herself up enough to kiss Jack on the cheek.

"I completely understand. I have to go use the restroom anyway. I think the coffee is getting to me."

"Do you want me to go with you?"

"No. I'm good, unless you have to go, too. If not, sit and relax. I'll be right back."

Aria stood and, after scanning the hallway, breezed out to find a restroom, wondering hopefully if there would be a repeat of her experience with Mr. Ross, or something like Mr. Ross.

Jack sat thinking he should have gone with her. After all, he could always go to the restroom, even if he didn't feel the need for it. He noticed the notebook on the floor, open to the last page on which Aria had written. He grabbed it and, still worried about the next interruption, started writing without taking time to read her entry.

*6:22 (I think)*

*I really do wish I could have been there to watch you bring someone back to life.*

*I hope you get to do it again.*

*Think about it. You and I, basically, already came back from the dead tonight. Someday, I think, we'll look back on all this and laugh.*

*We'll look back at you slipping off the bridge and me jumping in after you.*
*Honestly, I had no idea what I was going to do once I was in the water.*
*I think I just figured . . . well, I'm not sure what I figured.*
*But I know this—I didn't want you to be alone in the river.*
*Or maybe I didn't want to be alone on the bridge.*
*I'm just glad we ended up together, in the end. Well . . . not THE END.*
*At the barge, I mean. Jeez. I don't know what I'm talking about.*
*I'm just glad we're here. Together.*
*And I'm not sure what any of this has to do with you bringing someone back to life.*
*But I know that it does.*

Aria returned from the bathroom to find Jack writing the last sentence.

"What are you writing about?" She asked flatly, then gave Jack a mischievous half-grin.

Jack groaned at her tease. She knew it was a question he'd hoped to never hear again, at least not if he was writing in a bar, or coffee shop, or anywhere in public. Aria plopped down next to him on the floor.

"Hey, I know we need to get out of here soon, but can you do me a favor?"

"Anything."

"I'm getting really sore, and I know it's not just from this tile floor." She flashed a wry smile at Jack. "Can you look at my back?

I'm sure there are some bruises back there and just want to know the damage."

Aria turned away from Jack and lifted her shirt. Her back had been damaged by her time in the river, and Jack again noted the welt he'd seen when she lifted her scrub top in the exam room. But there were other scrapes and bruises, just not as prominent. He felt guilty about the beating she'd taken in the river and inched toward her wounded torso, figuring the ratio of unmarred to marred skin was about 50/50. He touched one particularly blue bruise, giving it a little push with his finger.

"Ouch! Okay, you found one. How's it look back there?"

"It looks like you fell off a bridge into a river and then ran into a barge, but I think you'll recover. I'm glad you took an Oxycontin."

Jack carefully started pulling her top back down.

"Can you do me?"

Aria finished lowering her shirt while Jack raised his and they traded positions. There was a long, scrapy bruise on Jack's back that covered nearly the entire center from below his neck to the top of his buttocks, as if he'd been dragged over a roll of barbed wire.

"You've just got the one back here. But it's big. Really, really big."

Aria traced her finger along the scrape before lowering his shirt and wrapping her arms around him.

Jack allowed Aria to pull him into the embrace and took a moment to enjoy it.

"Let's get out of here."

# Chapter Fourteen

## In God We Trust

Jack and Aria stood behind the storage closet door, preparing themselves to leave their safe haven. They'd grown comfortable in the dim light and quiet, finding themselves and each other among the hand soap and wash cloths and trash bags. Had they thought it safe, they would have opted to stay for another hour. But in their whispered chat they agreed it was important to get out of the hospital without being noticed, or at least being noticed as little as possible. In order to do that, however, they needed to find their clothes. As yet they had no solid plan on how to accomplish either, but knew they had to do *something*...or at least *begin* to do *something*. They couldn't continue nesting in a closet, no matter how much they desired to do exactly that. So they found themselves poised at the door, Jack gripping the handle in one hand and Aria's arm in the other.

"Wait!"

Aria blurted out the word and moved around to face him, taking his face in her hands.

"Kiss for luck."

Moments earlier, it occurred to Jack he really should take time and think it all through, that he should make a solid effort to put everything that happened—and what did *not* happen—over the last fifteen or sixteen hours into perspective.

He was making a mental note to that effect when Aria kissed him so, naturally, the mental note didn't stick. On the other hand, the kiss was heavenly, and they stayed in it long enough to build up a goodly amount of luck, long enough for their lips to tingle. Long enough to set their skin on fire.

Aria sighed and returned to her position behind Jack, wrapping him in her arms as he cracked the door open enough to peek through. Jack struggled to stay focused on the task at hand.

"Looks like we're clear." Jack grabbed Aria's hand and led her out of the nest.

They opened the door to the bright, sterile glare of the hallway and took a moment to orient themselves. The hastily concocted plan was supposed to begin with a search for their clothing, which meant they would be forced to return to the emergency room, and they were fairly certain that a trip to the ER would involve some sort of confrontation with the nurses, Deputy Lane, or both. It was a dilemma they would have to resolve, and so decided to play it by ear, as if they had any other choice.

"You sure this is a good idea?"

"Not at all. I was hoping for a flash of inspiration somewhere along the way."

Standing in the hallway, Aria and Jack recognized something had changed from when they first ducked into the closet, that all around them the energy and atmosphere were different. They were still alone, but knew instinctively they wouldn't be for long.

Jack gave Aria's hand a gentle pull and she followed him down the hall, walking briskly at his side. She recognized enough in her surroundings to know that if they didn't deviate from their route, the hallway would lead them back to the ER. She was going to say something to Jack when sanctuary appeared unexpectedly. It was a sign from above.

"Jack, look."

The sign said "Chapel."

Jack saw it too and veered toward the door, pulling Aria with him. They ducked inside, the door closing gently behind them. The lighting was similar to that of the storage closet, but the floor was carpeted and there were padded chairs instead of metal shelving. There was another difference as well. They were not alone. There was someone in the room with them, someone they recognized, even in the low light.

It was Father Randall.

He was on his knees, praying. His elbows rested on the back of the chair in front of him and he didn't seem to notice the arrival of his former ambulance mates. Aria thought he might be asleep, even though it would be nearly impossible to doze off in such a genuflected position.

*Years of practice?*

Father Randall's unexpected presence glued Aria and Jack to the doorway.

"Father? Are you . . . okay?"

It turned out the priest was not asleep. In response to Aria's inquiry, he lifted his head from where it had been resting on his hands and turned to the doorway.

"Ah, my young friends from the emergency room. To what do I owe the pleasure? Have you come to pray?"

Father Randall asked the second part of the question in a way that indicated he already knew the answer, but he waved them over anyway.

"Please. Sit with me."

Jack and Aria could find no reason to object. Father Randall, in their short time with him, had been more than pleasant, and surely God would welcome them as well. Father Randall lifted himself into a chair while Jack and Aria took seats next to him, Aria between the men. She took one of Jack's hands and held it tight against her thigh.

Father O'Neal turned toward his new seat mates. "Well, here we are. You probably wouldn't be surprised by this, but praying is one of my fortes."

Jack and Aria chuckled in recognition of the priest's joke, and Jack decided he should answer the question.

"Um, no, Father. We're not here to pray . . . not exactly."

The priest paused. "Young man, you don't have to tell me why you walked through that door. But unless one of us can come up with another topic of conversation it's going to be very quiet in here."

Aria was the first to confess. "Well, honestly, Father, we sort of ducked in here to avoid someone."

The priest rolled his eyes and chuckled. "Are you referring to the sheriff's deputy in the emergency room?"

Jack and Aria nodded, surprised by Father Randall's keen observational abilities and intuition.

"Well, my friends, if I'm being honest, I'll tell you that I'm here for the same reason. He was getting on my nerves about the blood alcohol test and I got tired of looking at him. He didn't bother me when I told him I was coming here, but who's going to tell a priest he can't go and pray in a chapel?"

He gestured with his arm, taking in the whole room.

"And this one's quite nice, I think. Very comfortable, especially compared to some other hiding places in the hospital."

Jack and Aria weren't horrified, but wondered if they should be. Was it possible Father Randall knew that their last hiding place was a storage closet? And that, on the floor of that closet, in the middle of a pile of linens, they had sex? They looked at each other, certain they were both thinking the same thing.

*No, there was no way he could know about any of that. Unless . . . Harvey? No way.*

Regardless, Aria decided it was time to change the topic. "So, Father, is it bad luck if I ask what you were praying for?"

"Not at all, my dear." He flashed another smile at Aria. "Don't worry, young lady. Talking about it doesn't jinx it, like wishing on a star or blowing out birthday candles. I was just asking the good Lord to help me unload some of the anger I've been feeling."

For their entire lives, it had never occurred to Jack and Aria that a man of God might have an anger management issue, or really any burdens borne by ordinary men, for that matter. They had always imagined a priest's life to filled with a sort of supernatural communion with God, their days spent unraveling mysteries and seeking enlightenment, like rock stars or astrophysicists. It didn't make any sense that Father Randall, or any priest, would be forced to deal with the mundane of the day-to-day. And the priest seemed like such a happy drunk. Of course, now was not the time to share their confusion or questions. The irony of a priest's confession was not lost on them however, and out of respect, they remained silent until he was ready to speak.

"By the way, I have whiskey, if either of you would care to partake."

Startled from their respectful silence by the unexpected proclamation, Jack beat Aria to the punch.

"Yes, Father, that sounds perfect." Jack and Aria smiled. Somehow, pouring whiskey into bellies bereft of food—but full of wake-up drugs, oxy, and coffee—seemed like the perfect idea.

Father Randall, delighted, pulled an aluminum flask from a pocket in his cassock and handed it to Jack, who took a sip and offered it to Aria.

"Don't worry young lady, there's plenty for all of us."

"I think you're the most fun priest I've ever met." Aria took a pull and handed the flask back to Father Randall.

"Oh, well then, I'll take that as a compliment, however, I've known many in the clergy you'd likely find more amusing than myself. Too many to recount here, I imagine. These days, though, I know of few people who need a good laugh more than a priest."

Father Randall received the container back from Aria and sipped, allowing his last sentence to float in the air above their heads. Jack and Aria, now enjoying the sensational burn of the whiskey in their stomachs, figured there was some truth to the statement, but did not inquire further. Allowing the priest's statement to dissipate, they drank in silence, passing the flask between them. On its fourth go around, Aria begged off, not at all sure the concoction she was creating in her gut would be less a sovereign remedy and more a hell-broth.

"Father, can I ask you a question?"

"Of course, young lady."

"Do people who commit . . . commit suicide. Do those people go to heaven?"

The priest took a sip before answering.

"Well, that's quite a question, isn't it? I suppose the short answer, for me anyway, is yes."

"Are you sure?"

He nodded softly. Father Randall could see that Aria was visibly relieved and handed the flask back to her as if it were a shaman's talking stick.

"Thank you. Thank you, Father, for that." She paused. Jack put a hand over one of hers. "Okay, one more thing, I guess, if you don't mind."

The priest nodded. "Of course, dear."

"May I ask, well, can I ask why you believe that?" Aria handed the flask back to Father Randall.

"Well, I believe the good Lord understands that if one reaches a point where they want to take their own life, well, then that person is no longer really responsible for their own behavior. That soul has reached such a point of anguish that they no longer see things clearly. In a way, a kind of evil has befallen them, and what they need is God's love and compassion, not punishment."

He paused, sipped, and smiled.

"That's the God I believe in, the sort of God we can all really get behind."

Jack listened intently to the conversation, at one point working to convince himself he was justified, in the end, to throw himself off the bridge, and listing the reasons to do so. The list was not long, in fact, it could be boiled down to one word—Troy.

Jack found himself deeply regretting that he allowed himself to reach a point where he no longer felt his life was worth living.

*I'm exhausted. Tired of myself, mostly.*

He was not asked his opinion and was happy for that. He was not prepared to jump into this particular chat, or articulate anything going on in his brain at the moment. He was more than content to passively observe Aria grill someone with a good bit more experience in the areas of life and death than he or she did. So, instead of inserting himself, he pulled the notebook from his pocket as inconspicuously as possible, so as not to disturb a conversation Aria was clearly finding beneficial.

*6:45*

*You're talking with Father Randall right now and I think he's saying things you need to hear. Sometime, you'll have to explain all of that to me.*

*I am listening, though, or at least I was listening, before I started writing.*

*I was wishing I could have had this same conversation with someone a year ago.*

*But, you know, even if I had, maybe I wouldn't have been ready to listen.*

*I'm ready now. I think you are, too.*

*We'll talk more about it.*

*But I doubt we'll have time until AFTER we make it out of the hospital.*

*And what about getting out of the hospital?*

*I'll bring it up when you guys are finished talking.*

*Maybe Father Randall could give us a hand with that, too.*

*Does that sound crazy? That I want to ask a priest for help escaping from the law?*

*You know what? Maybe not so much. He's hiding from Lane, too.*

Jack put the pad down in time to catch Father Randall giving Aria a hug. She was teary-eyed and still had the flask in her hand and Jack wondered what had been said while he was writing. The tears appeared to be ones of relief, as opposed to sadness or stress, and he wished he hadn't missed the end of their conversation. He made a mental note to ask Aria about it as she and Father Randall ended the hug. She noticed Jack looking at her and she handed him the whiskey. This was his opportunity to discuss an escape plan.

"Father, you already know this, but we need to get out of here."

Jack paused to drink from the flask.

"I'm willing to bet they're wondering where we've gone, and they might even be looking for us."

"What are you worried about, my son? The deputy in the emergency room?"

"Well, sort of, yes, mostly because we're not quite sure why he seems to have it in for us. I mean, I suppose I understand the blood test and all that but does he really want to arrest us for falling off a bridge? I mean, doesn't that sound a little obsessive?"

"Well, I imagine he thinks there's more to the story than the two of you just falling into the river. I've got my theories as well...if you must know."

Father Randall's hint of a knowing smile was accompanied by a piercing stare into Jack's eyes. "I'm not going to pry, however, unless you'd like me to."

Jack hesitated, squirmed, wondering if he should go ahead and follow Father Randall and Aria into their little truth circle, but decided not to do so. He was feeling time pressured and wasn't sure how to even approach such a confession. Besides, the priest already appeared to suspect more than he was letting on.

"Thanks, Father. I'm not up for it right now, but if anything changes . . ."

"That's fine, young man. I'm happy to talk about an escape plan. Oh, and not to be rude, but perhaps you could tell me your names."

"Jack."

"Aria."

"Well, then, Jack and Aria, I'm Father Randall O'Neal. It's nice to finally be introduced. As to our predicament with the law, I believe my problem to be somewhat more straightforward than yours. For me, anyway, they seem only to want to find out if I had a little too much to drink before I left the funeral service I was officiating."

He paused, as if waiting for follow up questions. When none were forthcoming, he continued.

"I will admit to both of you, here in this chapel, that I likely did, and between the snow and the extra tipple or two, my car didn't handle as well as it normally does."

Aria spoke up. "What do you think will happen? I mean, with the drunk driving and all."

"Well, young lady, I suspect nothing. It seems the good Lord and a couple of nurses conspired to slow the process on my behalf. I imagine my blood will not prove very helpful to the police, in so far as their desire to charge me with a DUI. In fact, for all I know, there's a good chance I'm already free to go. I just needed to have a little chat with God before I left. But, before I do that, what is it that I can do for you two?"

Aria answered for both of them.

"Well, you're right about us needing some help with the deputy in the emergency room. He seems to have had it in for us all night. We either need to find a way around him, or come up with a story he'll believe."

"So, you're saying you intend to be something less than truthful with him?"

Either due to lack of sleep or the effects of the liquid in Father Randall's flask, it hadn't occurred to Aria she was telling a priest that she and her new boyfriend were planning to lie to the police. The admission embarrassed her but it was too late to change her story.

"Yes, I suppose so, Father."

Father Randall stared at Aria for a moment, deciding for himself how far he wanted to pry into what occurred with the young couple in the hour before he met them in the ambulance.

"Let's not dwell on what may or may not have happened with you two last night. Whatever happened, it ended up with both of you sitting with me in this chapel. Obviously, the good Lord intends for me to help you with your dilemma. So, first, let me ask you if there's any way the true story isn't as bad as you think."

Throughout the conversation, Jack felt a pressure building to come clean with Father Randall, who already had his suspicions about what was being hidden from him. Jack wanted to spill the beans and let go of all he'd been hiding and, before he realized it, he gave the priest an abridged version of what he'd been up to the night before. Even with all the alcohol in his system, he managed to relay a fairly chronological account of his crawl through the local bars of his downtown Cincinnati neighborhood. He was able to exert *some* self-control, however and left Aria out of the story as much as possible, unsure as to how much she might want Father Randall to know.

Father Randall listened closely to Jack's ramblings, waiting until it appeared the story was complete, which was the moment Jack paused after saying the words, "And then we hit the barge."

"Well, now. That's quite a story, Jack. I have many thoughts on this, of course, but must admit I have no idea where to begin, except to say the last thing you want to do is tell the deputy what you just told me."

Jack was confused.

"Are you saying I, I mean we, should lie?"

"Absolutely."

Aria released a giggle.

"Are you sure, Father? That just seems . . . like the opposite of what I thought you'd say."

"I understand, Aria, but think about this. I believe your story, but Deputy Lane may not. Even if he does, Jack would be admitting to getting very drunk and purposely jumping off the bridge. That truth will confirm what he already suspects, and that could turn out poorly for the both of you."

Father Randall paused before continuing.

"But I want you to look at it this way, Jack: What you intended to happen did *not* happen. Yes, you ended up jumping off the bridge, but not for the reason you had planned. You jumped off the bridge to save Aria's life, or at least that's what I believe. I don't think this is something for which you should be punished, and I'm sure He doesn't either."

"He?"

The priest pointed to the cross hanging on the far wall of the chapel.

"Yes, my young friends. He."

"So . . . lie?"

"Yes. And if you didn't have to recover your possessions, I would advise you to just sneak out, but I don't think you want to leave those behind, so you're going to have to confront the deputy and tell him a story. And make sure you both tell the same story."

"Now," Father Randall said. "Let's pray for luck."

He kneeled and Jack and Aria followed suit.

"Father in heaven, we ask that you look out for these two young souls, and to guide them safely home. We ask that Deputy Lane leave the hospital now, if he hasn't already. And we ask that, if the deputy is still here, that he be sleeping peacefully when Jack and Aria walk out through the emergency room. Amen."

Jack was impressed.

"Wow. Good prayer, Father. Really specific."

"I find it best to be unambiguous when I speak to the Lord. Takes out some of the guesswork." He gave them a wink and stood, excusing himself as he made his way out of the chairs.

"It's time for me to go, Jack and Aria. I believe there is a car waiting for me. I hope to see you again under better circumstances and wish you both well."

# Chapter Fifteen

## There But for the Grace ...

The void created by Father Randall's departure was palpable. Besides the fact his chair was empty, the chapel was now considerably quieter. Deafeningly so. Jack and Aria took the opportunity to examine their surroundings. The chapel, Christian but non-denominational, was designed to be simultaneously comfortable and reverential. Sounds from the busy hallway outside the door were incapable of penetrating the heavy door, unable to disturb anyone seeking comfort inside its four walls.

"Hey, do you mind if I, you know, pray a little bit?" Jack pointed toward the cross and kept his voice low in an effort not to disturb the surrounding quietude.

"Oh, no, of course not."

Aria kept her voice low as well.

Jack mimicked Father Randall, kneeled in front of his chair, clasped his hands and put his elbows on the chair in front of him. He prayed silently.

*Ok, God, we've been talking a lot this last year. Not sure if everything that's happened since yesterday is your doing or not. Either way, I should be thanking you. Except for the tasing and the chance I might go to jail, I think everything has gone as well as can be expected, especially with Aria. You know, now that I think about it, you probably kept me alive, even though I still went off the bridge. I mean, you probably kept me alive by sending Aria after me, or something along those lines. Well, but hey, I mean, who am I to try to divine God's purpose? Ok, I digress. Give me a sec . . .*

Jack took a deep breath and gathered his thoughts before continuing his conversation with a higher power.

*Without rehashing everything I just said about saving my life and all, it really would be great if I COULD divine what you want me to do next. And now that I think about THAT, I kind of get freaked out. I mean, what am I supposed to do after all this? Go to work Monday morning like nothing has happened? Jesus Christ, (sorry) how are any of us supposed to figure this stuff out?*

*Ok, I'm sure I'm not the first person to ask that question, and won't be the last, but can you maybe give me a little hint? You know, a sign, from . . . well, from you?*

*I'm sounding really whiny right now. Sorry about that. I should really be thankful I've made it this far. So, in all honesty, thank you. Especially for Aria. Other than not dying she's the best thing to happen to me in a very long time. I hope she thinks so, too.*

*Well, I guess that's about it for now. Don't worry, I've decided to keep on keeping on, so to speak. I won't go through that whole thought process, other than to say I realize I dodged a bullet last night, and I can do better to fix things.*

*Ok, that's about it, really. I mean for now.*

*Wait. Just want to say I second everything Father Randall asked for.*

*And don't forget that sign thing, please.*

*Amen.*

When Jack slipped off the front of his chair to his knees, Aria saw the notebook on the chair next to his, and grabbed it when he started praying. He didn't seem to notice, and she told herself she had nothing better to do while Jack was talking to God.

Aria quietly turned to the next blank page and made another guess at the time.

*Seven-ish*

*You're next to me, praying, and I'm trying not to disturb you. Not sure how long you'll be so I'll write as quickly as I can. The whole thing with Father Randall was crazy, don't you think? But, you know, if I think about it, our chance encounter with an injured priest isn't the weirdest thing that's happened to us tonight. In fact, it might be the least weird thing. Anyway, I wanted to tell you about my sister, who killed herself a few years ago. I don't know if you knew anything about that or not. I tend not to bring it up randomly. I've noticed suicide isn't*

*a generally acceptable topic of conversation, unless the conversation is theoretical. Then everyone's got an opinion. Everybody shuts up as soon as somebody says they know somebody who really did it. But then, I suspect, nearly everyone knows*

*someone, or knows OF someone, who's killed themselves. But I'm willing to bet they're like me, and don't bring it up much, at least not if that person was an actual family member, someone they loved.*

*Anyway, I can't remember if I've ever said anything to you about it, but I doubt it. On and off, since it happened, I've tried to let it go, to stop blaming myself. Not much luck there. But I need to own it, or at least part of it. I won't go into that now.*

*I'm not sure how long you're going to pray and I already feel weird about writing in front of you. So, here's what I'll say, for now anyway. It's not just that I care about you. I do care about you. But, after my sister, I couldn't have another one on my hands. I had to stop you. If I didn't stop you, I don't know if I could take that. Understand?*
*Enough for now. Looks like you're done.*


Jack slid back into his chair as Aria slid the pen into the notebook's wire spine.

"You and God doing ok?"

"Good question. I'd like to think so. Maybe a qualified 'yes?' We'll see how things go this morning."

Jack saw the notebook sitting on Aria's lap but said nothing about it. Anything she was writing was her business, he believed, and that if she had wanted to say any of it out loud, or have him read it, she would tell him. His own experience, from his first entry to his most recent, supported that belief. When she was ready to talk about it, she would.

It occurred to him, however, that writing in the notebook was a communication choice in and of itself, that whatever she'd put in there while he was busy chatting with God was something she was ok with him reading, likely something she *wanted* him to read.

"Did God give you any clue as to how we're going to get out of here?"

"Nope. Not yet anyway. I think we're sort of in one of the 'God helps those who help themselves' parts of our adventure."

Aria laughed and gave them both a once-over. Though the scrubs remained relatively clean, she could still detect the faint smell of the river escaping their skin and hair, and the short sleeves of the blouses revealed some of the damage they'd received during their short time in the river. Though bruised and bloodied, their winter coats and clothing appeared to have armored them from the worst the river had to offer.

"We still need to get our clothes, Jack."

"Ugh. I know, but I'm not looking forward to it. If it hadn't been snowing all night, I'd suggest we just slip out a side door somewhere."

"I thought of that, too. And that brings up another problem."

"What do you mean?"

"I mean we have no idea how we're getting home. It's a pretty long walk from here, even if it weren't freezing outside."

"Still a lot of snow out there?" Jack realized he hadn't looked out a window for hours.

"I'm guessing yes. It would not have melted overnight. Shoes would definitely make the trip a lot easier." Aria paused to think. "Ok, first things first. Let's find the clothes. After that we play it by ear."

Jack believed her "plan" to be somewhat lacking in detail but said nothing. Like cats with nine lives, they had so far survived every challenge of the evening, and he figured they shouldn't mess with success, or at least what could be reasonably referred to as "success." However, there was part of Jack that believed attempting to retrieve their clothes from a room full of people was asking for trouble, especially when those people were either waiting for their return or, worse, actively searching for them. He also figured the wet clothes had been trapped in the plastic bags for hours and, in those hours, unpleasant things like mold and nasty river bacteria had likely taken refuge in their porous layers of cloth. There was no doubt in Jack's mind that those bacteria were now actively reproducing, and his brain did not paint a pretty picture of pants and shirts covered with baby fungi and river stink. So, despite continued triumphs, Jack wasn't sure their clothes were worth the risk, and would have been happier had they thought of a way to forego their recovery, though he agreed shoes would be a good thing to have.

"I'm going to peek out the door and see how it looks out there."

Jack stood and walked to the door, cracking it open just far enough to get a good look at the hallway. It was empty, and he said as much to Aria.

She flashed him a mischievous smile.

"What are you thinking?"

Jack sat back down with Aria, who still had the notebook on her lap.

"You wanna fool around?"

Jack's mouth answered before his brain had an opportunity to think about it.

"Yes. Absolutely.

"But, crap, I think it would feel too weird in here. I mean, He's watching . . . probably." Jack pointed to the cross hanging on the wall.

Aria took his hand and leaned into him.

"You're right, and even if he isn't, we've got to get moving. But, one thing, lemme go find a bathroom before we go get our clothes. I'll be quick."

"No problem. Be careful out there."

Aria pointed to the notebook on the chair.

"Don't read that yet, okay? I want you to read it, just not yet."

Jack nodded. "Sure. Absolutely."

"Ok. Thanks, Jack."

She moved to the door.

"Be right back."

Jack started scribbling as soon as Aria was out of the room.

*7:15 AM (gotta be after 7 at least.)*

*Ok – I'm writing in the log but I want you to know I'm not looking at what you wrote.*

*And, you should know, that's not that easy.*

*The words are right there, not far from mine.*

*On a different topic . . .*

*I'm sitting here writing and every time I look up I'm looking at the cross.*

*I haven't been in a church since Troy's funeral.*

*It was rough. Charlie and Sarah (Troy's parents, in case I never told you that) barely looked at me. I was still banged up from the accident.*

*I was sort of in a wheelchair and couldn't escape. I wanted to escape.*

*Here's another thing. I haven't thought about Troy for the last couple hours.*

*Is that awful of me? I feel guilty about that. I don't think I'm allowed to not think of him.*

*Ok, I'm going down a rabbit hole here. I'll change the subject again.*

*Let's talk about us.*

*So, not to go all religious on you, but I'm starting to think all this was fate.*

*I mean, maybe not hardcore fate, like when everything is absolutely preordained.*

*I'm talking about, I don't know, more like "fate lite," you know?*

*Maybe when just a few things were meant to happen.*

*Make sense? Probably not. I'll try to explain.*

*I'm starting to think I was supposed to spend this time with you.*

*I'm starting to think something will come of it. Something good.*

*Honestly, I don't know how it couldn't. But there is a downside to all this excitement.*

*If this is our first date, there's no way the second one will be as interesting.*

*We'll have to set the bar lower for the next one.*


The door opened just as Jack closed the notebook. Though the door was almost silent, the swish of it startled him. He turned quickly, fearing the worst, and breathed a sigh of relief upon seeing Aria.

"Coast is clear, as far as I can tell."

"Any problems finding the bathroom?"

"Nope. Found one of those family restrooms. Had the whole thing to myself. It was quite spacious."

Aria spied the notebook sitting on Jack's lap and had a moment of panic. "Reading or writing?"

"Writing. I kept my promise."

"Thanks," she smiled. "Now let's get out of here. When I came back there was no one in the hallway, so I think we stand a good chance of getting to the ER without getting noticed."

Jack grabbed the notebook, forgetting all about his own need to urinate, and worked his way through the chairs to get to Aria. He was still ambivalent about returning to the emergency room, but willing to trust his fate to the universe.

"Ready." He took a deep breath.

"Follow me."

Aria opened the door, peeked out and didn't see anything. She grabbed Jack's hand and gently pulled him into what she believed to be an empty hall.

The hall, however, was not empty. As they turned out of the chapel, they were immediately confronted by Nurse Rita, who was as surprised as they. However, being Nurse Rita, she recovered quickly from the shock of seeing her errant patients wandering the hospital hallways.

"And what have you two been up to?"

Her demeanor was more inquisitive than stern, especially compared to their earlier encounters.

Jack and Aria started blathering, interrupting one another in their attempt to explain the series of events that led to the moment Nurse Rita caught them coming out of the chapel. The words flowed from their mouths, yet they managed to avoid saying anything about their excursions to the gift shop, the pharmacy, or the storage closet. Nor did they mention how Aria helped to save an old man's life, or their desire to avoid Deputy Lane.

"Well, the waiting room you sent us to was empty . . ."

"Yeah, and then we waited and waited . . ."

"And we even fell asleep, you know, because we were waiting for so long . . ."

"Right, and then, you know, when we woke up . . ."

"It was still empty, so then, right, then we decided to come back down to the ER . . ."

"Yeah, we decided to come back down, but we got turned around somewhere . . ."

"And we found a coffee machine, and somebody gave us some money for the machine . . ."

"So, we drank some coffee and, you know, figured out which way we had to go . . ."

"Back to the emergency room, and then, we saw the chapel . . ."

"And Father O'Neal was there, so we talked to him for a while . . .

"And then he left and, well, here we are."

Nurse Rita looked skeptical.

"So, basically, you're telling me you took a nap in a waiting room, got some coffee, and then started praying?"

Aria and Jack nodded fervently.

"Alright, well, just so you know, your blood tests came back and while they showed you both have, or had, alcohol in your systems, it was below the legal limit. We gave the deputy the results but I don't know if he's still there or not.

"Listen, my shift is over, and I'm not really in the mood to take all this, whatever all this is, any further. I don't know what happened up in the psych waiting room, but you wouldn't be the first people to get forgotten so, if it's all the same to you, if you two can convince me you're not going to hurt yourselves, I'll make sure all of this gets dropped."

Aria tried her best to project a demeanor of innocence.

"Honestly, Nurse Rita, we never intended for things to go this far. Nearly everything that happened last night was just a weird, freak accident. And then you and the other nurse started asking us all those questions from the suicide thing and, well, I can't speak for Jack but I found them a little confusing, and we're tired, and our answers, I think, were coming out weird . . ."

Nurse Rita cut her off.

"Alright, Aria, alright. You can stop right there. We're fine. You're fine."

Nurse Rita looked them up and down and almost laughed. Standing before her were two disheveled individuals who had clearly been through the wringer, and she took pity on them.

"When's the last time you two ate anything?

Aria and Jack thought back, trying to remember the last thing each had eaten, finally concluding their last meal was lunch the day before, and let Nurse Rita know as much.

"Wow, ok. You two come with me. I'll buy you some breakfast."

Jack and Aria, due to successive periods of emergency, stress, distraction, and drugs had managed to stave off hunger longer than they'd realized, and the thought of a meal overwhelmed their focus on recovering their clothing and getting out of the building.

"Follow me."

She stepped past them and, after a moment of hesitation, Jack and Aria followed her down the hallway. The passageway was unfamiliar, and busier than the ones they'd roamed the last few hours, looking for the pharmacy, bathrooms, and coffee machines. They knew it was likely that all the hallways were busier than they had been earlier. They could feel the whole building waking, refilling itself with staff, patients, and families.

The new energy, in one way, was exciting, and the sun streamed in on them from large windows. Their night spent in the windowless bowels of the hospital hid from them the changing conditions outside the building; Jack and Aria did not know the sun had risen, and they felt its energy augment the pharmaceuticals and coffee they'd consumed earlier. Their steps lightened.

But there was a downside to the people and the sunlight. They were getting looks. During their time in the hospital they had forgotten they might look out of place, walking around in socks, hair unkempt. But the looks mostly went to the socks, and then disappeared. Jack noticed and, looking around, realized half the staff appeared as if they themselves had just rolled out of bed. And it wasn't like the hospital's visitors were arriving in formal attire. It was early for them, too.

They knew they must be close to wherever Nurse Rita was taking them. The smell of bacon—the pied piper of culinary aromas—greeted them in the hallway, beckoning. Just a few yards more and they were standing in line behind Nurse Rita in the employee cafeteria. Jack and Aria were still getting a few looks but, apparently, Nurse Rita commanded a certain respect among her coworkers and none questioned why she was taking civilians through the employee line.

Jack and Aria could barely contain themselves, filling their plates with more bacon, eggs and toast than they could possibly eat in one sitting. Nurse Rita paid for their bounty with the promise they would return to pay her back at a future date. She did not expect to be repaid, however, at least not by these two. The universe would reward her, she understood, and expected never to see Jack and Aria again, believing in the future they would likely work to avoid this hospital, and all hospitals generally.

The three found an empty table and ate their meal. Nurse Rita still had questions, though far less weighty than the ones she'd asked them earlier. She wanted to know what would become of them, but was not inclined to interrupt the polite but rapid inhalation of food taking place across the table. Had she not had food in her own mouth, she would have laughed at the ravenous display. She waited until the intake slowed before striking up a conversation.

"What's next for you two? Where do you go from here?"

The question, to Jack and Aria, sounded more ominous than Nurse Rita intended. *What was next?* Their plan, as flimsy as it was, had been interrupted by Nurse Rita herself. In concentrating on the immediate task of filling their bellies, Jack and Aria had temporarily forgotten their (hopefully not impossible) mission of retrieval and escape.

They looked at each other, and Aria responded for them both.

"Well, I suppose the first thing we should do is find our clothes. We were headed back to the ER when you saw us in the hall."

Jack nodded in agreement. "Yes. That's what we were doing."

"Well, I think I can help you with that. When you didn't come back after we sent you upstairs, we cleaned those two exam rooms for other patients and moved your stuff to the intake desk. It's still there, waiting for you."

Jack and Aria thanked Nurse Rita while they cleaned their plates.

"Do you want more?"

"No, no thank you. You've done enough for us already. I think we can take it from here."

Jack really meant that, too, even though they had yet to implement their shoddy escape plan.

"Well, alright then. I'm going to get home to my family, and I suggest you both do the same."

Nurse Rita stood, took her tray to the trash can, waved at Jack and Aria, and walked away. Her absence from the table made them feel self-conscious. Their shield was gone, and the stares seemed more apparent, even if they weren't.

It was time to go.

# Chapter Sixteen

## The Sun Also Rises

Having eaten, Jack and Aria felt better, but now blood rushed to their stomachs, clearing their extremities, including their brains, and soon they felt overwhelmed by fatigue. Though all eyes were definitely not on them, they *felt* as if they were. The self-consciousness was acute, at least it was until they took a moment to examine the people sitting around them. Other than not needing a shower quite as badly as Aria and Jack, those in the dining room shared aspects of their appearance. In addition to the ubiquitous scrubs and white coats, there was the obvious lack of sleep. There were those whose shift was just starting, but maybe had partied too hard the night before, but most appeared to be those whose shift just ended, those who spent the last eight or sixteen hours working with few or no breaks. Realizing just how much they blended in, how their attire and exhaustion had become forms of camouflage, they relaxed and plotted their next move.

But it was still time to go.

With a nod of silent agreement, they grabbed their to-go coffee cups, emptied their trays and shuffled out of the dining room.

Jack and Aria stopped outside the cafeteria, sharing a moment of hesitation. They knew they had to go but, all in all, felt things hadn't gone too badly since they'd arrived hours earlier. After all, they'd made friends with some of the staff, discovered they were physically compatible, successfully self-medicated, and rediscovered their faith in humanity through the actions of a janitor, a priest, and a nurse. For what more could they have asked?

Aria nodded in the direction of the emergency room.

"You think he's still in there?"

"If I had any money, I'd be willing to bet on it."

"Stick to our story?"

"Stick to our story, just like Father Randall told us to do."

Jack gave Aria a kiss for luck (it had worked so far,) but made it quick, fearing a prolonged public display of affection might draw more looks and break their tenuous cover as "staff."

"We'll be okay, I think. I mean, think about it. We've kind of kicked this hospital's ass."

Aria laughed and took Jack's hand.

"Alright. One more hurdle."

Aria was feeling borderline fatalistic, as if the river was still carrying her, but she was ready for whatever was coming next. Shuffling toward the emergency room, holding Jack's hand, her brain replayed the last eight hours and she silently checked off, one by one, all the times something could have gone drastically wrong but somehow didn't. She wondered if they, or anyone, could really be that lucky in the face of such long odds.

"It doesn't matter." She unintentionally released the words as a whisper.

"What's that?"

"Oh, nothing. I'm good."

She squeezed Jack's hand and leaned, just a little, into his shoulder.

With the hospital coming alive around them, they did not hurry. The rising energy in the floors and walls did not penetrate the peculiar cocoon they'd created around themselves as they walked patiently toward the emergency room, where their dirty clothes currently resided, and where they would confront a rash of faces they would not recognize. The next shift had begun while they took refuge in the chapel and shared breakfast with their former nemesis and one-time interrogator, Nurse Rita.

When they reached the door to the ER waiting room, they paused a moment and looked at each other. The sunlight filtering through the glass doors and windows lit their faces, crowding out the fluorescent glare to which they'd grown accustomed. Jack looked through the window, and could see him. Rather, he could see the hat.

"He's there."

"Well, crap. Stick to our story, right?"

"Right."

Jack used his free hand to open the door. They were only steps from where Deputy Tommie Lane slumped, passed out in a chair close to the intake desk. Jack led Aria toward the sleeping figure, but she resisted, halting their forward motion and slowly mouthing her thoughts to Jack.

"Let's—just—go—around—him."

Jack thought for a minute and came to the conclusion that going around the deputy was only a temporary solution. They'd spent the last few hours evading the inevitable, or at least some of the inevitable, or at least this part of the inevitable. Even if all they were going to do was lie, they needed to tell the lie. Deputy Lane could not be avoided. If they tried it would just come back to bite their asses, and likely later in the day, once they were home.

Jack imagined the deputy finding out where they lived and concocting some excuse for tracking them down. Upon locating them, he would, almost certainly, launch into another interrogation, basing it on some wild theory about their suspicious behavior and possible criminal intent.

Jack decided not to share his trepidation with Aria, lest she consider him paranoid, and therefore less than capable of maintaining any semblance of a stable relationship.

He shook it off.

"No, I think it's better just to get this out of the way."

Aria nodded, fighting the instinct for flight over fight. "Okay."

They were standing behind the snoring deputy, who was clearly well-practiced at chair-sleeping. Aria reached out, and gently touched his shoulder. Other than to stop the snoring, the effort had no effect, and Deputy Lane continued a shallow, REM-type breathing. Aria looked up at Jack, shrugged her shoulders. Jack responded by nodding toward Deputy Lane.

*Try again, please.*

Aria reached out again, grabbed the deputy's shoulder and shook him. This time Lane responded, jerked forward and stood quickly, his blank gaze scanning the surrounding area in an attempt to determine the threat. When his hand reached for his gun, Jack and Aria hit the floor.

Seconds later, Deputy Lane was fully awake, his eyes settling on Jack and Aria, formed into a ball on the floor in front of him while several startled ER staff froze in their tracks, uncertain as to what was happening.

"What the hell are you two doing?"

They looked up, hoping the threat had passed. They didn't really understand the question. Maybe Lane was still confused. Why would he be asking them what they were doing? He'd been on the lookout for them for hours. He just reached for his gun. Had he forgotten that?

"The gun. You reached for your gun."

"We thought you were going to shoot us."

Deputy Lane stared down at his hand, which was still gripping the handle of his holstered service weapon.

"Oh, shit. Sorry about that." The nearby staff relaxed and normal ER activity resumed.

Jack and Aria slowly rose to their feet, eyes on the deputy, who stepped back a little as he released his pistol.

"Can we explain?"

Lane nodded and Jack began.

"Okay, well, we saw you sleeping there and, you know, we just figured you wanted to talk to us before, you know, we left."

Aria chimed in.

"Yeah, before we left, you know, of our own free will."

Deputy Lane stared at the man talking to him, the man he'd chased and tased just hours before, wondering why he and the girl hadn't just left and gone home while he was asleep. After all, he'd already received the blood alcohol results from that mean nurse and they were too low for him to make a case for something along the lines of a drunk in public charge. The only reason *he* was still there was exhaustion. He figured he could catch a few winks before driving home. But, then again, there was still the other thing. He pulled himself together.

"Okay. Fine."

The deputy's eyes darted back and forth between Aria and Jack.

"Why don't you tell me what you'd like to talk about?"

It was clear to Aria and Jack that the good deputy was still confused or, perhaps, dissembling, and they decided to play along with whatever game he was playing.

"What we'd like to talk about? Oh, nothing in particular, I guess. We were told we could leave, so . . . that's what we were doing, and then we saw you in here, sleeping."

Deputy Lane's intense stare made Aria nervous.

*Does he know something he's not telling us?*

Not in the mood to listen to Aria ramble on about whatever it was that motivated her to wake him up, Lane felt the need to direct her narrative.

"Okay then, why don't you tell me, exactly, why you found it necessary to wake me up?"

Jack waded back into the conversation.

"Well, you know, like she said, you've been out here all night, waiting for alcohol tests, or whatever, and we just wanted to make sure your business with us was done before we left. I mean, no offense, the last thing we want is you knocking on our doors later today, looking to 'bring us in' or whatever. See what I mean?"

Aria nodded.

Deputy Lane had seen this behavior before: the meandering speech pattern, the half-assed conclusion that trailed off into silence. It had all the hallmarks of someone who was self-medicating. Or they could just be exhausted, like him.

"Are you two on drugs?"

Aria involuntarily crossed and uncrossed her arms. The deputy was staring at her again, after having taken a break from her to stare at Jack.

"What do you mean?"

The deputy seemed unimpressed with Aria's response, but his body language remained passive.

"I mean, are you two on drugs? You know . . . drugs? Chemicals you take that make you feel weird; make you do weird things; make you say weird things? You know. Drugs."

Jack leapt to Aria's defense.

"Well, how do we know you're not on drugs?"

"What? What are you talking about?"

Lane felt the situation deteriorating rapidly and wanted to avoid any more confrontation with the couple standing in front of him. Pausing to regain control, he took three deep breaths, the way he'd been taught in that anger-management seminar. In between his second and third breath, Aria started speaking again.

"Sorry about my friend here, Deputy, I think we're all very tired."

Aria tried to speak in soothing tones, the way she did with drunk and/or unruly bar patrons, but to Jack and Deputy Lane her voice just sounded stilted, like she was trying to breathe and talk at the same time. "I think what he's trying to say is, well, I think he's trying to say you've been here the whole time. We would definitely not try to take drugs while you were here . . . watching us."

Deputy Lane was ready for Aria to stop talking, but she seemed incapable.

"But it's not like we go around taking drugs when there's no cops around. I don't mean that. You know? But we definitely wouldn't do drugs while you, or any cop, were around us. I mean, that would be dumb, right? Again, not saying we go around doing drugs. I'm just saying that we certainly wouldn't do them in front of a cop, you know, I mean, if we did them. Which we don't."

Aria laughed nervously. Jack shrugged and nodded as if the proof of Aria's statement was self-evident.

"Besides, it's not like we can just walk into the hospital pharmacy, grab some drugs and walk out again, right?

Deputy Lane was nearly as tired as Jack and Aria and had given up, right around the third sentence, trying to make sense of Aria's helter-skelter response to his drug question. He was verging on not listening at all by the time she rolled around to the bit about the pharmacy. His motivation to get to the bottom of their story waning, Lane decided to dramatically speed up the process before he no longer cared.

"Listen, you two. At the end of the day, I don't really give a crap if you're on drugs or not. What I really want to know, what I've really wanted to know all night, or morning, or whatever, is what you two were doing on that bridge in a snowstorm, and how you ended up in the water. If one, or both, of you can answer that one damned question, we'll all be good."

Jack and Aria glanced at each other, surprised and rather pleased with the bluntness of the inquiry. As fortune would have it, the opportunity for them to deliver their well-practiced lie to Deputy Lane had finally arrived. They took a collective breath, reminded themselves of the simple story, and pushed it through the cobwebs of their memories.

But nothing happened. The words, by now trapped in errant, burned-out synapses, refused to emerge.

Deputy Lane, unimpressed with the pregnant pause, pointed at Aria.

"You. Start talking."

The command startled Jack and Aria out of their clogged thoughts, and had the salutary effect of knocking the words out of Aria's brain and into her mouth. But they weren't the words she'd been planning.

"Well, it started yesterday, when Jack came into Liberty's, where I work, to have a drink and write in his journal."

205

Jack recoiled at the truth. Actually, he recoiled at the fact that, for reasons he didn't understand, Aria appeared to be sharing totally unnecessary information. They had agreed on the lie. They had agreed, over and over again, on the lie and here she was telling the truth, as if they had no plan at all.

More damning, at least to Jack, was the fact she'd referred to the Drunk Log as a "journal."

*It's not a stupid journal. It was supposed to be my last words, not some record of how my day was going, of how so-and-so or what's-her-face hurt my feelings at lunch.*

It took Jack a few moments to recover from Aria's error in nomenclature and refocus on what she was saying to Deputy Lane. She was moving quickly, without pause, through the story of her search for Jack, and he found himself unable, or perhaps unwilling, to interrupt or interject. Until that moment, Jack was ignorant of most of the details of Aria's search for him. So, he did not get in her way, suddenly, unexpectedly, engrossed by the description of her evening, of the things she encountered, of her search and rescue. He was especially struck by how close she'd come to catching him *before* he got to the bridge, and how she'd seen many of the things he'd seen, often just a few minutes separating their witness.

Deputy Lane remained quiet as well, astounded at how easily the truth had emerged and patting himself on the back for trying to pay attention in Psych 101. He did not interrupt her, confident he was getting all, or at least most, of the story, now markedly different from the one they told the night before.

When Aria was done, the deputy looked at Jack, who was staring at Aria and who had not said a word.

"What about you?"

Before responding, Jack took a moment to take in Aria. She was standing next to him, facing the deputy. He could see the tears making tracks down her cheeks. He was not angry with her for telling the truth. He couldn't be. He was too relieved to be angry. She had decided for them, decided they would tell the truth, no matter the consequences. She would tell him later that it had to be that way, that they couldn't start the next part of their relationship, whatever it was going to be, on a lie.

"I wanted everything on the table," she told him.

When it was his turn, he tried to be as courageous as Aria, and told his side of their story as concisely as he could, leaving out only the parts he actually didn't, at the moment, remember. The two of them had by now been awake for more than a day, so some amnesia was to be expected. There were difficult moments, when he spoke of Troy, when he spoke of his guilt. In those moments he pulled it together and continued his confession, continued to unburden.

Aria took in every word, found it ironic and almost amusing they were both bearing their souls to a hardhead like Deputy Lane, as if he were now wearing two hats—the cop doubling as the therapist.

When he was done, Jack felt significantly lighter, and wondered why he hadn't done this in the last year, wondered why he waited until that moment to confess his guilt to a priest and a cop in succession. And he knew the answer. Fear. Fear of letting anyone in. Fear of being shunned in his daily life the way he'd been shunned by his family.

Deputy Lane listened to Jack as intently as he'd listened to Aria, and with the same confidence in the fidelity of their version of events. He wanted to know more, not to build a case, but simply because he was fascinated by what he was hearing. But fatigue was affecting his attention span. When Jack paused, the deputy waved him off, letting him know he didn't need to say anything else.

"Listen, you two. I'm tired, and I'm inclined to believe everything you're telling me, even though I'm a little pissed that you didn't just tell me, and everybody else, the truth when we first asked you about it. You could have saved me a lot of trouble."

Jack and Aria glanced at one another and Jack made a feeble attempt to explain their behavior.

"Yeah, well, we are actually really sorry about that. We just had no idea what you guys were thinking, or if we'd done anything wrong, and what kind of trouble we'd get in if we had done something wrong. . . ."

Deputy Lane cut him off again.

"Listen to me for a minute, okay?"

Jack and Aria nodded, ready to listen.

"So, here's the thing in a nutshell. You told me you went down to that bridge to kill yourself, right? But that wasn't the reason you jumped, right? You jumped because your, well, your . . . I don't know. What are we calling her?"

The deputy pointed at Aria.

"Girlfriend. I'm his girlfriend."

Aria answered before Jack had the chance.

"Okay, fine. You jumped because your girlfriend slipped on the ice and went over the handrail, right?"

Jack nodded.

"Okay, so, like I said, you didn't jump because you were trying to kill yourself. You jumped because you wanted to help her, your girlfriend, which, I think, was pretty courageous. I'm not going to arrest you for being brave."

Deputy Lane paused for a moment.

"But, I gotta say this—I have no idea what you thought you could do once you were in the water, in a freezing cold river, in the dark, not knowing what was up or what was down. You were really lucky to hit that barge. But that doesn't matter. My point is that I'm not going to arrest you for trying to be a hero."

Jack nodded, feeling some sense of relief that he and Aria had spilled the beans. He wasn't sure how to respond to someone who called him "courageous" for something he'd done on instinct. It was fine that he didn't try to speak, however. Everything that had happened was starting to crash in on him, and he felt it quite possible that, had he tried to speak, he would have broken down right there in front of his new girlfriend and a cop he'd basically detested until five minutes ago. In lieu of speaking, Jack held his hand out to Lane, receiving a quick shake for his trouble.

Other than having asserted that she was, indeed, Jack's girlfriend, Aria maintained her silence as she observed the interaction between Jack and Deputy Lane. One of the things she'd learned in the last few years was that if things were going your way, let them. And things were definitely going their way. Of all the potential outcomes that could have befallen them since they went off the bridge, each turned out to be benign. Each turned out to be something they hadn't needed to fear, no matter how dire things looked in the moment. She wasn't sure exactly why but, as she listened to Jack and Deputy Lane, she suspected their good fortune resulted from some sort of heavenly intervention, that fate had determined the consequences of their actions would be minor.

*Or maybe we just outlasted everyone.*

It occurred to her they were being released simultaneously from the clutches of the law *and* the medical system, due to some combination of luck and sheer endurance. She liked the thought. It would make for something to write about.

"Is it okay if I hug you?"

Aria, too, was feeling a bit gushy. She felt the conclusion. She could feel the *end*, at least to this part of their time together, and though she wasn't sure she actually cared for the young deputy, she was at least willing to forgive, and to mark that forgiveness with a light hug.

Lane, still somewhat confused, allowed himself to be embraced. Awkward hug complete, Aria remembered she had one more question for the lawman. "Was Father O'Neal okay when he left the hospital?"

"No idea. *He* wasn't my problem." Lane smirked at Aria, making sure to remind her that *she and Jack* had been his problem. "But I think I saw him leave a while ago. Somebody came in and walked him out to a car."

Deputy Lane tipped his hat to Jack and Aria, turned, and walked out the door, into the sun. The snow had stopped a couple of hours earlier, leaving a crisp layer of white on nearly everything Jack and Aria could view through the glass of the automatic doors. In the last few hours, they had forgotten the "outside" existed, and the sight of it reminded them they would have to re-enter it soon enough.

Aria hugged herself. "Jeez, still looks cold."

Jack thought so, too. "Let's get our clothes, and then try to figure out how we're going to get home."

Aria stared out the glass a moment longer. "Definitely. I don't think we can walk from here; not in socks, anyway. Do you think there's such a thing as 'scrub shoes?'"

Jack laughed. "I think they're called 'crocs.' But I don't think they'll give us any."

They were only a few steps from the front desk, the place Nurse Rita said their bags were stashed. The intake desk was now occupied by someone they didn't recognize.

"Excuse me, nurse? We were told our clothes were being held at this desk. Should be two plastic bags of stuff?"

The nurse pulled the two bags out from underneath a corner of her desk.

"Do you have any ID?"

Jack and Aria shared a slight panic. Any identification they had was inside those plastic bags with their certain-to-be-smelly clothing.

"Just kidding. I know who you are."

She handed the bags to Jack and Aria.

"And don't worry about the scrubs. Consider them our parting gift."

Jack and Aria took the bags, tried to laugh at the nurse's joke.

"Thank you."

"Wait!" Jack handed his bag to Aria. "I'll be right back."

He scooted back to the emergency room, to Aria's former exam room. After making sure it was unoccupied, Jack gently opened the curtain and found what he was looking for. There, on the chair next to the bed, was the teddy bear he'd gotten for Aria from the gift shop, the one Harvey told him he could take.

The bear had been moved to the chair from the bed when the room was readied for the next patient.

"Here. I didn't want to forget this."

"Thank you, Jack."

Aria hugged the bear and gave it a kiss on the forehead.

"I don't want to spoil the moment, but we have to think about something else."

"How to get home?"

"Yep."

Jack sat next to Aria in the waiting room. By then the Modafinil had lost much of its potency and exhaustion was creeping in. The problem of getting themselves home, given their lack of cell phones and ability to remember anyone's phone numbers, was a big one.

As they silently pondered their options, the automatic doors opened with a gust of cold air and sparkling powdered snow, in the midst of which stood Deputy Lane, appearing like a vision in the blinding morning sunlight. He gazed around the waiting room and, as he cleared the doorway, spotted Jack and Aria.

"Hey, you two. Need a ride?"

Aria giggled and whispered to Jack.

"This is the universe solving our problems for us."

Not having been privy to her metaphysical thoughts on their situation, Jack could only nod and pretend he knew what she was talking about.

Aria jumped out of her chair with a smile.

"Yes, please, officer. That would be wonderful."

Jack and Aria tucked their bags under their arms and followed Deputy Lane out the door into the bright, white morning. He turned to them and pointed to the only sheriff's cruiser in the parking lot.

"I'm right there.

"By the way, how long have you two been dating?"

# About the Author

**Mark E. Scott** lives in the Over The Rhine neighborhood of downtown Cincinnati.

*Upcoming New Release!*

## FREE WILL
### A DAY IN THE LIFE SERIES
#### BOOK THREE
#### BY
# MARK E. SCOTT

Jack and Aria stand outside the emergency room in wrinkly scrubs and wet non-slip socks, looking more like a commercial for the Salvation Army than the lovebirds they've become. Thus far they've deftly managed to avoid getting arrested or locked in the looney bin. Now all they have to do is figure out how to get home.

Over the next eight hours, Jack and Aria dive deep into their individual histories of loss, grief and guilt between catnaps, snowy hikes for food, and being stalked by a reporter determined to find out what really happened to them the night before.

This dark comedy builds on the themes of *Drunk Log*, Book One and *First Date*, Book Two, the continuation of *A Day in the Life*, and follows our protagonists to the conclusion of their search for love and redemption.

**For more information**
**visit:** www.SpeakingVolumes.us

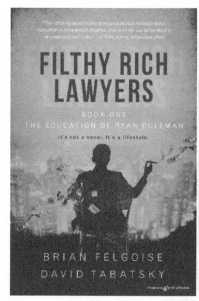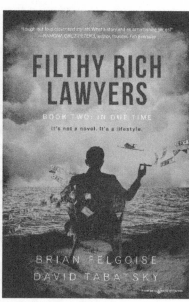

*Now Available!*

# JAMES V. IRVING'S

# JOTH PROCTOR FIXER MYSTERIES
## BOOKS 1 – 4

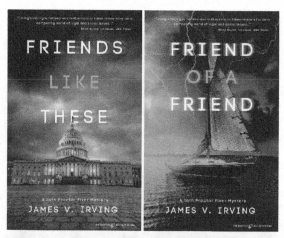

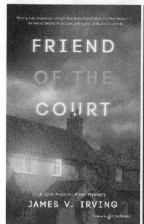 

**For more information
visit:** www.SpeakingVolumes.us

Made in United States
North Haven, CT
07 July 2023

38675899R00136